Sinners and Saints: Sword of the Gods

P.B. Holcomb

<u>Trigger Warnings</u>

This book contains several graphic and disturbing things that may not be suited for all readers. Please see the below triggers and make sure you are alright to proceed before reading. While I hope you enjoy this book, your mental health matters.

- Strong Language
- Alcohol Use
- Graphic and Detailed torture and death scenes against women
- Violence against Children
- Death of Children

<u>Dedication</u>

To My Darling Wife, Christine and Our Beautiful Son, Dean

Neither I nor this world deserves the light you provide us. The strength and love you give to me each and every day could never be repaid in a thousand lifetimes. You are now, and forever will be, my reasons. Without you, there is no me.

Christine, you are my rock and my shelter through the deadliest of gales. In nineteen years together, you have been my defense and shield. You have backed my decisions, even when the decisions I made turned out to not be the right ones. You are my reminder that true love really does conquer all.

Dean, the wonder and zest with which you approach this world is my inspiration. You have reinvigorated my spirit in times when I've felt I have nothing left to give. I continue on because I know that in the end, you will always be my greatest accomplishment, and that one day I will leave this world in your capable hands to continue on my legacy. In the words of Tim McGraw, "When you get where you going, don't forget to turn back around. Help the next one in line.
Always stay humble and kind."

Prologue

1947

The night was bitterly cold on the lonely South Boston street where St. Augustine Catholic Church stood. The wind whipped furiously, and the flurries danced around so wildly that it looked like the whole area was trapped inside a recently shaken snow globe. Inside the house of worship, Sister Catherine McNeil was kneeling, lighting a prayer candle, and preparing to bow her head when a loud series of knocks sounded at the main entrance. The elderly nun slowly rose and shuffled her way across the crimson carpet to see who on Earth could be out on such a nasty evening. The weather and temperatures were so bad that night that Father Hansen had canceled the evening mass. Just as she reached the double doors, the knocks thumped again, echoing through the empty auditorium. She cracked the door just enough to answer it, keeping out as much of the chill as she could.

Outside stood a tall and stout-looking man of about thirty-five in a black trench coat and gray fedora. Sister Catherine was taken aback at the man's intimidating size, and even more so by his

appearance. He was broad shouldered and had an extremely thick neck to match. His hands were rough-looking and oversized, so that they more closely resembled bear paws than hands. Still more off putting was his face. Even though the brim of his hat was pulled fairly low in the front, she could see a large scar running from just underneath his left eye down to his jawline. It was plain to the nun that this was a wound resulting from a past altercation with another person. How else would a man this large and brutal-looking receive such a scar? Still, she put her best foot forward and, in a
meek and polite voice, asked, "How may I help you, young man?"

The man smiled broadly at the nun, revealing his bright white teeth, except for two on the upper left that had been replaced with gold ones. In a thick Russian accent, the man replied, "May I please come inside, Sister? The night is so cold that it almost reminds me of my homeland."

Sister Catherine hesitated for a moment, but then said to the stranger, "Of course, my child. I'm afraid Mass was canceled tonight, but you're welcome to come in and warm up for a moment if you wish. You're always welcome to pray while you're here as well." She stepped aside so the man could enter.

"Thank you, Sister," the man replied as he stepped inside and closed the door behind him. As he shook off the cold, he continued the conversation. "Sister, I didn't come to attend Mass. I was hoping to speak with Father Hansen. He's an old friend of mine, and I was hoping to catch up with him for a bit."

"I'm sorry, young man," Sister Catherine stated apologetically, "But Father Hansen is currently in his office studying and has asked not to be disturbed. I would be happy to take your information and let him know you wish to speak with him when he's available. Perhaps you could stop by tomorrow if you're in the area."

The man wore a slight look of disappointment. "Well, that's too bad. I was looking forward to seeing him. I'm leaving town tomorrow, so this was my only opportunity to visit with him. Are you sure there's nothing you can do?"

She apologized to the man once again and said, "Sir, as I stated before, you're welcome to stay for a few minutes and pray if you wish, but other than that, it is getting rather late, and we'll need to start closing up shortly. If your business is concluded here, I respectfully request that you leave. May the Lord God keep you and watch over you on your travels."

At these words, the big Russian's demeanor suddenly changed to one of disapproval and anger. He glared intensely at the nun for a moment, and then turned his mouth up into a sickeningly twisted smile that made Sister Catherine audibly gasp and step back a few paces. He reached out with one of his massive arms and grabbed hold of the older woman by her throat. His hand was so big that his fingers completely wrapped around her neck. He squeezed down with vice-like strength and lifted her off the ground until her feet were dangling beneath her. "Your God does not keep me, old woman! Your worthless God is dead to me, no more than an afterthought." The hulking man threw Sister Catherine backward with tremendous force, and she toppled head over heels across the rearmost row of pews. As she fell, she smacked her head on the back of the next set of pews. She lay there for a minute, dazed and dizzy, trying to get to her feet.

Before she could stand, the Russian was on her again. She attempted to scream, but he put a hand over her mouth, and the sound came out as more of a muffled whimper. The man slammed her down onto her back, laying her across the seat of the pew. His eyes went wild, and he produced a wicked sneer on his face as he wrapped both of his huge hands around her neck and began to choke her. He began to chuckle to himself as the frail nun tried to fight him off, smacking his arms and pushing against his face with her bony fingers. He took his time with her, enjoying every moment by releasing the pressure just enough to let her take in a decent breath, and then crushing down again on her throat. Eventually, his joy subsided, and he decided that Sister Catherine's purpose had run its course. He violently pressed in on her neck, and the sheer strength was such that with one loud pop, the nun's spine was shattered and her body went limp. The man arose and looked at what he had done. "Worthless cunt," he exclaimed as he spat on the lifeless woman.

Back in his office, Father Hansen was studying and preparing for the next day's mass. He had just finished reading the verse, "Be sober, be vigilant, for your adversary the devil walks about as a roaring lion, seeking whom he may devour," when there was a light knock on his office door. He stood from his chair, walked over to the door, and opened it. There was no one there. He stepped out into the hallway that led from his office into the auditorium. He looked around for a moment, confused, and then asked, "Sister Catherine?" There was no answer. As he turned to walk back into his office, he felt a sharp, momentary pain on the back of his head, saw a blinding white light, and then, darkness took him.

He awakened groggy yet aware, feeling cool, rough concrete against his cheek. He looked around and quickly realized he was in the cathedral's basement. The pain in the back of his head and neck was almost unbearable. He had no clue how he had gotten there, that is, until he heard a voice.

"Welcome back, Father Hansen," the Russian said mockingly. The priest turned around, still in a prone position, to see a gigantic man towering over him. "I was beginning to think I may have hit you a little too hard, and that I may not get to speak with you."

Father Hansen gathered his thoughts as best he could and asked, "Who are you? What do you want with me?"

The man just shook his head and said, "Who I am isn't important. As for what I want, I do want something, but not you. Rather, it's something that you possess that brings me here tonight. As you can see from the state of your basement, I am in a bit of a hurry." The priest looked around the dark, slightly damp room to see that stored items had been tossed around, that there were papers strewn all across the floor, and that boxes had been dumped.

"What are you looking for?" Father Hansen asked. His tone was unsteady, and his voice began to tremble.

"Don't play dumb with me, holy man!" The Russian swung his arm forcefully and backhanded the priest. Hansen's head snapped back from the blow. The large man grabbed the priest by his hair and slammed him down into a nearby chair. "You know what I'm here for. I've searched this entire fucking building, and it's nowhere to be found! But I know that you have it hidden somewhere, and you *will* tell me."

"You'll never get away with this," the priest yelled while pointing an accusatory finger at the man. "You may be able to hide from the justice of man, but you cannot hide from the judgment of God!"

In one swift motion, the Russian grabbed Hansen's extended digit and snapped it like a toothpick. The priest howled in pain. "It's not polite to point at people, Father," the man laughed. "This is only going to get worse for you if you don't cooperate," the Russian said with a tinge of frustration in his voice. "Now, let's try this again. I'll speak more plainly. Where is the fucking amulet?!" He grabbed hold of another one of the priest's fingers.

"God will protect me. You have no sway over me. Even if you kill me, I'll go to the arms of the Father, and you will go to your appointed place in due time," Hansen said flatly. There was another crack, another splintered digit, and another howl of pain.

The man slapped Hansen hard across the face again and gathered the priest's arms behind him. He took some black plastic zip-ties from a bag on the floor beside the chair and bound the father's wrists to the metal seat. "I'm running extremely thin on patience, Father. Tell me where the amulet is, and this will all be over. At which point, I'll be more than happy to send you to the false god you love so much."

The priest averted his eyes and said nothing. He watched as his assailant rummaged through the bag and produced a small sledgehammer. He then grabbed a handkerchief from his coat pocket and tied it around the priest's mouth to act as a gag. "Father, you're in the basement of a church where no one can hear you. Oh, that's right. I forgot to mention to you that your bitch of a nun who refused to let me speak to you is lying dead on the pews. I snapped her neck like a twig. It was so fun watching the light leave her eyes, Father. So, no one is coming for you. There's no help. There's no escape. God and everyone else have abandoned you."

At the news, Father Hansen's eyes welled with tears, and they slowly trickled down his face. After a few moments of breaking down, the priest began to mumble. The behemoth Russian removed his gag, and as soon as he did, the priest began to recite the Lord's Prayer. "Our Father, who art in heaven, hallowed be thy name..."

The man shook his head in disbelief for a moment, but then laughed a full-bellied laugh. "I'll say this, Father, you've got balls...or rather, you did!" He replaced the gag and, without warning, brought the hammer down with extreme force directly between Hansen's legs. There was a sickening crunch, and a wet spot immediately formed on the priest's pants. He couldn't even manage a scream, as he almost passed out from the pain. The Russian smacked the priest's cheek several times to keep Father Hansen awake. "Stay with me, Father, we're almost done."

It took several minutes of deep breaths for the priest to compose himself, and then he mumbled something to the man. The Russian, thinking Father Hansen had finally succumbed, leaned in close to hear. "Thy kingdom come. Thy will be done, on Earth as it is in heaven."

The man growled loudly in anger. He began to go around the room, throwing random objects in a fit of rage at the priest's resolve.

The priest's voice grew louder. "Give us this day our daily bread, and forgive our trespasses as we forgive those who trespass against us. Lead us not into temptation, and deliver us from..."

The Russian, overcome with blinding hot rage, finished the priest's words, shouting, "Evil!" He began swinging the hammer wildly, raining blow after blow down on the priest. The gray stone walls and floor quickly turned red as every hammer strike shattered bone, sinew, brain matter, and other bits of the helpless priest. Even after the priest had long since expired, the Russian continued to swing until there was virtually nothing left of the father's head and upper torso. Finally, exhausted and covered in gore, the man stopped his onslaught. He composed himself, cleaned off as much of his task as he could, and reclaimed his trench coat and hat.

Just as he was about to walk away, he took one last look at the priest and then at a spot about three feet behind. He almost couldn't believe it. In his rage, he hadn't seen it fall. Yet, there it was. The amulet's golden hue glowed faintly in the room's low light. The gold chain attached to it stood out like a sore thumb against the bloodstain. The bastard had been hiding it in plain sight this whole time. It was around his neck and had been flung off during the brutal attack. The Russian laughed insanely as he picked it up and wiped it clean. He placed it around his neck and began to ascend the stairs that led back to the auditorium. As he left the basement, he paused and looked back at Father Hansen's mutilated corpse. He said mockingly to it, "When you meet your precious God, priest, tell Him I'll be sending Him more of his children very soon." He then climbed the stairs, exited the church, and disappeared into the bitterly cold night.

Chapter 1

Present Day

The cell phone lit up, vibrated, and began to dance across Buddy's nightstand. Groggily waking like a surgery patient coming out of anesthesia, he muttered the words, "Are you fucking kidding me?" as he began to fumble around, trying to grab it. As he did, all he managed to accomplish was to accidentally knock it behind his headboard and onto the floor beneath the bed. "Really?" he grumbled, flipping himself over angrily and reaching underneath the bed to search for the phone. Finally grasping it, he rolled over onto his back, squinting from the bright light to look at the contact info. The screen read, "SAC Charlie Seavers." With an audible huff and an eyeroll, Buddy swiped the green "talk" button and held up the phone to his ear. "Barrett," he said in a flat tone.

"Hey, Bud," Special Agent in Charge Charlie Seavers said in a reserved tone.

Buddy huffed again. "Charlie, it's three in the damn morning. We haven't spoken in six months. What possible reason could you have for calling me right now?"

"Yeah, sorry about this, Bud. I know I should have called more often to check on you, but work has been crazy, and with everything you've gone through and are still going

through, I just thought you might need some time, you know?"

"Yeah, I get it, Charlie. Let's cut the bullshit, though. What's going on?"

Charlie let out a frustrated sigh. "Bud, I've got a problem down here, a big fucking problem, and I could use your help. I know you're technically on an open-ended leave of absence, but..."

"Charlie, you're rambling. Get to the point."

"Maybe I shouldn't have called. This was a mistake."

"God, damn it, Charlie, spit it out! I'm tired, and my patience is wearing..."

Charlie interrupted forcefully, "It's happening again."

The rest of Buddy's rant hung in his mouth, and he shot straight up in bed as if he had just been struck by lightning. He sat there with his mouth hanging open, his lungs paralyzed and unable to take in air. There's no way Charlie could be talking about

15

what Bud thought he was. This couldn't be happening, not again. His ears began ringing with a high-pitched buzz, and he could feel his heart thumping against his chest cavity with a steady, rapid pulsing. He could hear something muffled around him, but it was incoherent, that was, until Charlie's voice finally shot back into focus.

"Bud! Answer me, damn it! Are you still there? Are you okay?"

Buddy shook his head for a moment to clear the cobwebs and ran his fingers through his salt and pepper hair. "Uh, yeah. Sorry Charlie. I'm, I'm still here."

"Damn, Bud. You freaked me out for a second. You sure you're okay?"

"I said I'm fine, Charlie," Bud snapped, even though he clearly wasn't. "What do you need from me?"

"Can you meet me at the office first thing in the morning? I've got some things to go over with you. I need your advice. I know it's a big ask, but I don't have anyone here who has even half of your experience and knowledge on this case."

Buddy was silent for a few more moments, lost in his thoughts. "Yeah, Charlie. I'll be there."

"Thanks, Bud," Charlie said sheepishly. "I owe you one, partner."

Buddy disconnected the call and tossed the phone on his nightstand. In his haze, he didn't realize he had slung it a little too hard. It skittered across the wooden surface until he heard the distinct ting of glass. He glanced over and noticed the half-empty bottle of bourbon sitting beside the phone. His head fell into his hands, but only for a moment before he reached over, uncorked the bottle, and took a slug of the potent amber liquid. He resealed the container and set it back on the stand. With a long-winded sigh, he rose and made his way to his bathroom. As he did, he paused momentarily to gaze out the big bay windows of his studio apartment.

The Kansas City skyline was engulfed in darkness, with the only light coming from the windows of other buildings, stretching out like tombstones in a massive cemetery. The darkness was then suddenly broken up by a brilliant flash of light and the unmistakable clap of thunder. As he walked on, rain began lightly wrapping against the glass in an almost soothing pattern. He could hear the wind whistling in a hushed tone, like a new mother trying to calm a restless baby. Another bolt of lightning flashed, signaling that the storm was getting closer and stronger. He broke his blank gaze and continued to the bathroom. He placed his palms down and leaned over the sink. Looking at himself in the mirror, he let out another mournful sigh and then picked up a bottle of Ibuprofen. He downed a couple of the brown pills and made his way back to sit on the edge of his bed.

He sat there for a few moments, replaying the words over and over again that Charlie had spoken to him. "It's happening again." Without warning, vivid images began to flash in his head: the pools of blood all over the beige carpet; the same sticky, crimson substance covering his hands. He began to hyperventilate. More images came: a vision of him holding the cold, lifeless bodies; the red and blue flashing lights of the police cruisers. He broke into a sweat. Still more images bombarded him: first responders rushing into the room, and being pulled away by his partner, Charlie, as his wails of pain pierced the air. Buddy felt the dizziness begin to overtake him, and then darkness followed.

He awoke with a start, screaming, "Susan! Lilly!" The alarm app on his phone was blaring out the same annoying little tune it always did. Wiping the sweat droplets from his brow, he slowly reached over and shut off the alarm. He sat there for a moment in silence, and then burst into uncontrollable sobs as tears began to stream down his face. It felt like his head was on fire as he sat there holding his face in his hands. But after what felt like an eternity trying to gather himself, he finally came to his senses. He stood up slowly and went for a shower. He adjusted the water temperature to as hot as he could stand it, a habit he had picked up after showering with his wife all those times. They even had a running joke about it. She liked her showers so hot that Buddy used to tease her that he felt like a lobster being boiled. Now, though, he didn't feel right taking them any other way. He stood there letting the water run over his face and shoulders until it almost went cold, trying to wash away the nightmare that had plagued him this morning, just like so many other mornings. He stepped out, walked over to the sink, and wiped away the steam with his hand. He stood there for a moment, staring at himself.

He mumbled to himself, "Jesus, Bud. Thirty-five isn't supposed to look fifty." He shook his head in disbelief. However, his self-assessment was a little unfair. Although his face *was* a little haggard from lack of sleep for extended periods, Special Agent Bud Barrett was still quite a physical specimen. Standing six feet four inches tall and weighing a solid two hundred and thirty pounds, he had always been a little intimidating to those around him. His muscled body was lean, not bulky, something he had always strived for in his daily workouts. Even when he was in the Marine Corps, he preferred flexibility, agility, and range of motion over brute strength. He regularly thumped the meathead powerlifters in his unit during hand-to-hand combat exercises because he could always out-maneuver them.

He was also, according to his girlfriends in his younger days and to Susan all the years after, "quite a handsome man," though Buddy himself would never admit it. One unique quality about him that people always seemed to point out was his salt-and-pepper hair. He developed it from a fairly young age, a trait his mother had told him he had inherited from his father. Buddy never got to see this for himself, as his father had died during a routine training exercise on a helicopter during his time in the Marines. Nevertheless, he had always received a mix of both ridicule and compliments for it during his youth. As he matured, he learned to embrace it. Plus, it was a stark contrast to his piercing emerald-green eyes, the one feature he enjoyed about himself. After all, it was the first thing Susan had noticed when they met, and it was what ultimately got him out of trouble most often when she got upset with him. All of these thoughts had been swimming through his mind as he gazed into the mirror, wondering how so much of himself could have been changed in such a short amount of time.

He walked over to his closet and slid open the doors. He stared for a moment at the black, tailored suits hanging there. He grabbed one out and took it off the wooden hanger. It took him a few minutes to adjust to wearing it again. Part of him thought he might never put it back on in an official capacity. He had wrestled so hard with himself this entire time over whether or not to leave The Bureau that he had physically exhausted himself at some points. Yet, here he stood, staring at himself in his FBI garb at his full-length wall mirror. He couldn't help but chuckle to himself as he thought about all of the movies and TV shows that he had seen over the years that depicted FBI agents as overbearing, narcissistic assholes. The stereotypes weren't *completely* baseless. He knew several agents at the Kansas City office who fit the bill. Buddy could always sniff out those guys, the ones who either didn't have a military background or, at best, had just enough discipline not to get dishonorably discharged. He had always strived to be the best version of himself that he could be. After all, that's what a Marine did: work towards perfection in all things.

He then walked over to his bed, got down on his hands and knees, reached under it, and pulled out a heavy black lockbox. He pressed his thumb against the scanner plate on the lid, and it popped open. He peered down into the box. His Franklin 19M sidearm sat tucked neatly inside. He hesitated for a moment before picking it up. After six months of not even looking at the weapon, it felt foreign, yet somehow familiar and comforting in his hand. He turned it over, remembering all the grueling hours he had spent at the range to become an expert marksman. After all, real life wasn't like the movies. Most civilians just assumed that agents were born with a gun in their hands, ready to kick ass and take names like the job was some shitty action film. No, it had taken him years to perfect his craft, split between his time in the military and during his training to be an FBI agent. He popped the fully-loaded magazine into the bottom, pulled back the slide to place a round in the chamber, and stood to slide it into the holster on his right hip. The weight of it felt good to him after a few steps, like a part of his body that had been missing was suddenly reattached.

Walking over to his chest of drawers, he slid open the top one. He retrieved his wallet, car keys, and badge. He didn't even glance over at the black velvet box, which also lay in the drawer. It contained the Purple Heart he had received from his time in Afghanistan, when he was shot in the shoulder during a mission to push back a group of insurgents that had entrenched themselves on a mountainside. He never acknowledged the award. He held firm to the belief that the only Marines who deserved to be awarded were the ones who never made it home. He slid the drawer closed. As he did, a photo sitting in a sterling silver frame on top of the chest gave him pause. He picked it up and stared at it intently. The photo was of a beautiful blonde woman kneeling in a lush, grassy field before a large oak tree on a cloudless summer day. In her arms was an elementary-aged girl in a laced white dress, her mischievous grin wide as she hugged the woman in turn. A single tear ran down Buddy's face and splashed onto the picture.

"Don't worry about me, girls. I'm gonna be okay. I love you and miss you so much, and I promise you that I'm gonna help Charlie find that bastard and make him pay for what he did to you. Either that, or I'll be seeing you both again very soon."

Chapter 2

Buddy arrived outside the Kansas City field office about five minutes before nine o'clock. He stood uncomfortably, staring at the grey stone building with oversized bay windows above the front entrance. He blankly stared at the American flag gently rippling in the light breeze, which was also surrounding his face as it brushed past him. He was quickly brought back to reality when a light vibration against his side signaled a phone notification. He reached into his pocket and checked his cell. There was a text message from Charlie. "Hey, Bud. Got your message. Be out in just a second." He returned the phone to his pocket, took a deep breath, and walked up to the front doors. After clearing the security check-in protocols of the building, he stood there anxiously waiting for his old partner in the large lobby.

His eyes were on the floor as he was again lost in thought when he heard a familiar voice. "Boss?" the voice asked, confused. It was a woman's voice. Buddy looked up to see Special Agent Mya Alvarez staring at him with wide eyes and a beaming smile. Buddy hadn't seen Alvarez since the night that his wife and daughter were murdered. Hers was one

of the last faces that he saw that night, along with
Charlie's, as he was being questioned during the
debriefing after leaving the crime scene. She had
worked directly under him as a probationary agent
for a couple of years, and then again as his new
partner when Charlie got promoted to SAC.

Intelligent, tough, strong-willed, and street-
smart, Alvarez was the daughter of Mexican
immigrants. That probably also explained her fiery
side, since Buddy had met her mother a couple of
times and found her to be just like her. Buddy had
heard several stories from some of the other probies
about her insane work ethic and anal-retentive nature
during academy training. Buddy imagined that was
because she had to be that way. Standing only five
feet and six inches tall and weighing about a buck
twenty-five soaking wet, she was forced to work
twice as hard as everyone else to succeed. She was
also always extremely well-groomed and buttoned-
up, never having a single strand of her hair out of
place.

Buddy liked her from the moment they met.
Most importantly, he liked her because she was a
former Marine like him, and secondly, because she
was never afraid to speak her mind. Even with senior
agents, she didn't put up with any crap. The first
exposure he had to her was in one of the break
rooms as she was engaging in some locker room talk

with some of the other probies. As he was walking up, one of the guys had made an off-color comment about her being flat-chested. She fired right back by saying, "That's funny, dude, but my chest still isn't as flat as the front of your crotch." That sealed it. From that moment on, a friendship was born between the "two old jarheads," as she liked to joke.

"Alvarez, how the hell are you?" Buddy said with a light smile.

"Better than you, Boss. You look like shit," she quipped back.

"You're not wrong," he replied with an almost inaudible chuckle.

"What the hell are you doing back? I thought you were out on leave."

"Agent Seavers asked me to come in for a chat."

"Oh, shit. That can't be good. That means something's up. It makes sense, though. Seavers has been walking around here with a stick up his ass for a couple of days, but hasn't told anybody why yet."

Just then, Charlie's voice rang out. "Agent Barrett, good to see you again." He extended his hand.

"Well, hello, Special Agent in Charge Seavers," Buddy fired back in a mocking, but light-hearted tone.

"Alvarez," Charlie said as he nodded at Mya.

"Oh, my God. You guys are so dumb. You act like we don't already know each other," she snipped, as she shook her head and rolled her eyes.

"That's what I love about you, Alvarez," Charlie said. "You're never one to mince words."

"Well, I guess I'll leave you two boys to your meeting," Mya said.

She was beginning to walk away, but Charlie called to her. "No, Alvarez, I need you, too. Even if Buddy is on leave, he's still your partner. Let's head up to my office, and I'll fill you both in on the details."

They made their way to Charlie's office, and once inside, he shut the door behind them and drew the blinds for privacy. Charlie then walked to his desk and unlocked the top drawer. He reached inside and slapped a large file folder onto the wooden tabletop. All three of them stared at it for a moment before Alvarez finally broke the silence as per usual. "Holy fuck," she said in a hushed tone. "Is that what I think it is?" She picked up the folder and opened it carefully. She looked at the main tab. It was labeled, "Unsub 1325, aka: The KC Crusher."

The "KC Crusher" was what the press had labeled him after the first three victims were found. All of them were young, attractive females who were also active within the Christian church, albeit in different denominations. Their bodies had been found dumped, unceremoniously, in alleys and side streets in the Kansas City area. Their bodies were so bent, broken, and tortured that they were only able to be identified through dental records and DNA comparisons. Buddy remembered each of the first three victims vividly.

The first victim was Mandy Sloan. She was twenty-five and a Sunday School teacher for St James Episcopal. A short, petite blonde, her extremities had been pulverized to the point of being gelatinized with a blunt object. She was then decapitated perimortem, meaning that she was alive while her head was being removed. This act of obvious psychopathy was the spark of Buddy's obsession with solving the case.

The second victim was Jamie Sykes. A twenty-two-year-old college student at Baptist Bible College, she aspired to become a full-time missionary to the Philippines upon completion of her studies. That dream was cut short, however, when the unsub kidnapped her after a late-night campus bible study.

Witnesses described her as a "fiery, spirited redhead with a zest for life." She was also taking self-defense classes at the time of her abduction. None of this mattered, as she was found several days later in a culvert not far from the campus with a shattered pelvis and a broken neck.

The third victim was Maggie Taylor, a twenty-seven-year-old homemaker and mother of three. She was the choir director at Faith Church of Christ in the downtown area. She was taken in broad daylight from a local grocery store, only to be found the next day by a homeless man looking for cans and other recyclables to trade in for cash. She was found with her spine completely snapped in half, her body folded backward at the waist. However, this victim in particular is what sealed it for Buddy that they were dealing with a potential serial killer. Unlike the others, this woman had a message cut into her body from the base of her neck down to her pubic bone. It read, "Bog mertv," which, in Russian, loosely translates to, "God is dead." "Charlie, why do you have this file out?" Mya asked.

Charlie looked at the other two with a somber yet serious expression, especially focusing on Buddy. "Because, Alvarez, he's started up again."

"Shit. Are you sure it's him?" Mya asked, almost in disbelief.

Charlie nodded. "Almost positive. Local LEOs have found two adult females exactly one week apart with the same cause and manner of death. It's his M.O., Mya. Both women were pulverized to the point of being unrecognizable with a blunt object. Buddy, that's why I called you to come in today. You were the lead on this case before, well, everything happened. You know this unsub inside and out. Please confirm my suspicion before I reform the task force. I'm sorry to ask, but I want to make sure these weren't isolated incidents or a copycat."

During the entire conversation, Buddy hadn't taken his eyes away from the folder. He was staring a hole through it. His worst fear had come true. He was going to have to face his worst nightmare all over again. He looked up and sighed. "Charlie, what is it that you need me to do?" He was asking a question he already knew the answer to. He wasn't here for a consultation; Charlie wanted him back in the field. He was going to ask Buddy to investigate the two homicides. He wanted Buddy back full-time to hunt down the madman who, to date, not counting these two possibles, had murdered forty-five women in the span of a little over two years, including Susan and Lilly. Buddy swallowed hard and slumped back in the chair he was occupying.

"Who else knows about this, Charlie?" Bud asked.

"For now, it goes as high as the Assistant Deputy Director. We're not running it any higher up the flagpole until we confirm and figure this shit out," Charlie responded.

They all sat in silence for several minutes, each gathering their thoughts. The tension in the room was palpable. It was as if they were all experiencing a shared déjà vu, frozen in the same moment. Finally, Charlie looked knowingly at Buddy and then at Mya. He said, "Mya, give us a minute, would ya?" Mya respectfully nodded and left the office, gently closing the door behind her. As soon as she was gone, Buddy spoke.

"Charlie, I already know what you would ask of me, and believe me, I want to help, but I don't know if I can..."

Charlie replied, "Bud, I can't imagine what you must still be going through every day with this shit-storm in your head. Susan was like the little sister I never had after you two got married, and Lilly was the best of all of us. I miss them, too, man. Look, I know you're crushed inside, and I would never assume to know your mind on this, but I do know one thing. You want this asshole off the street so he can't hurt anyone else the way that he hurt you and your family. Tell me I'm wrong, and I'll let you walk away from this permanently. But I know you, Bud.

You're a good man and a good Marine. You protect people. It's what you were born to do."

Buddy took a deep breath and replied, "You're right, Charlie. I was a good man, and I was a good Marine, but when it came down to where the rubber meets the road, I couldn't protect the two people that mattered most to me in this fucked up world." A single tear welled in his eye and then rolled down his cheek. "I was supposed to always be there to protect them. I was their hero, Charlie, but I let them down. I got so wrapped up in the fucking case that I didn't see it coming. I pushed too hard; so hard that the fucker found out too much about me and took away from me my only reasons for living." Buddy stood up and made his way over to one of the big bay windows in the office. He peered down for a bit onto the street below, and then continued. "Damn it, Charlie, I don't know how to do this without them. You're right. I do want this guy off the street. I want him to pay. I want him to suffer. I want to visit upon him tenfold the pain I've gone through. I don't know how to start again." He hung his head and leaned against the windowsill.

Charlie walked over to his old friend and placed a hand on Buddy's shoulder. He leaned into Buddy's ear and spoke softly, "You start the only way Marines know how, my old friend. You focus on one mission at a time, and fuck shit up until something makes sense. You're not alone, Bud. I'll make sure that Alvarez and I are right beside you, fucking shit up, too. We're gonna find this asshole, man, and this time, dead or alive, he's done hurting people. Semper Fi?"

Bud wiped the tears from his cheeks, looked up at his old partner and friend, and in a shaky but determined voice, returned the call. "Semper Fi."

Chapter 3

The hum of the air conditioning unit beside his black sedan had begun to eat into his brain. He had been sitting in the driver's seat for far too long, and his ass was getting numb. This was the most excruciating part for him-the waiting. It always had been. He had already been here for almost two hours. He wondered to himself how anyone could sit and listen to the mindless bullshit about God's love and protection for this long. His only comfort in this current holding pattern was the darkness that enveloped him completely on the side street to which he was currently parked. He took in a deep, cleansing breath as he pondered this. People may lie about who they were to their friends and family, but no one could lie to the darkness. The darkness was purifying. It was when everyone's true motives became clear, because the darkness could hide their true nature from those they wished not to see it. Like the fires of hell cleansed sinners of their transgressions for an eternity, so too did the darkness shield the deeds of those who were truly wicked at heart.

Yet, what was wickedness? Wasn't wickedness a subjective term? When most of the sheep who claimed to be God's children defined wickedness, it was described as misdeeds such as the so-called "Seven Deadly Sins" of lust, greed, envy, sloth, gluttony, wrath, and pride. He smirked to himself and shook his head. It was laughable at best because most of these hypocrites were guilty of every single one of these things and more. Not only did they commit these sins, but in his eyes, a sin far worse: judging others and condemning them under the guise of piety and self-proclaimed tough love. He, however, had seen this folly at a very early age and decided that he would be the one to put a stop to the fallacy of it all. He set his jaw and furrowed his brow. The darkness was to be revered. It never judged, but only allowed people to be who they truly were inside without fear of persecution from those who would compel them to suppress their true desires and beliefs.

The doors of St Matthew Presbyterian Church suddenly burst open wide. He raised his binoculars to get a closer look. Some children began running down the main stairs, their parents trailing lazily behind, conversing as they shuffled. Pastor Wilson also emerged into the entryway, shaking hands with congregation members as they exited the large white building. The red double doors of the main entrance were a stark contrast to the rest of the building. Probably some rubbish about representing the covering and protecting Blood of Christ. He became nauseous at the thought. The exodus continued for about 15 minutes. It set his teeth on edge watching from afar, knowing what his ultimate goal was this night and the euphoria it would bring him. He was almost levitating above his seat with anticipation by the time the last few people left. Then, he saw her.

She glided out of the doors like she hadn't a care in the world. He raised his binoculars again. As he watched her chat with the pastor, he felt his pulse quicken and his energy rise to a fever pitch as the moment to make his move approached. He knew what came next, having watched her perform the same routine every Sunday morning and evening, and every Wednesday evening, for the past three weeks. She would finish her chat, bidding the pastor a good night. He would leave, and she would walk back inside to tidy up the pews before coming back to the front and locking up. She was such an obedient and loyal little dog, making sure that God saw all of her good little deeds for a possible pat on the head in the afterlife. It began to rain as he watched her lock the crimson doors and walk across the parking lot to her car. It was time.

He quickly started his engine, drove across the street, and into the church parking lot, making sure he was methodical enough not to alarm her. He could see her digging through her purse for her keys as he stopped about a car's length in front of her. She looked up at him. He made sure to leave on his high beams to blind her from seeing his face. He wasn't worried about her escaping, but if, by some miracle, she did, he didn't want the added attention of being identified. He slowly opened his car door and stepped out, staying by it to bolster her perceived security.

He called out to her in his Russian accent.

"Laura Kelly?" "Yes? Can I help you?" she replied.

"My name is Detective Alexander Petrov with the Kansas City Police. I was told I could find you here."

"What's this about?" she asked hesitantly.

"It's about your husband, Jimmy. He's been involved in a shooting incident. He's stable, but badly injured. He's currently at Mercy Hospital undergoing surgery. I came to escort you to him and ask you a few questions upon our arrival. Time is of the essence."

"Show me your badge," she said flatly.

"Of course," he replied. "May I approach?"

She nodded, and he walked up to her slowly and carefully. He reached into the inner pocket of his black trench coat as if reaching for his badge. She carefully watched him, but it was too late, and he was too close. In one swift, fluid movement, he pulled the miniature billy club out of his coat, smacked her across the back of the neck, and caught her as she fell. He looked around quickly to make sure no one was watching, and scooped her up in his massive arms. He popped the trunk and roughly tossed her in and closed it, but not before rummaging through her purse to find her car keys. He parked her car a few streets over, just to confuse the idiot police who would eventually come looking for her, and then walked back to his own and left the lot.

A half hour's drive later, he pulled up to the abandoned textile factory on the outskirts of the city. This was his sanctuary, the place he did his glorious work. Like a still undiscovered painter longing for recognition and prestige, he would paint another masterpiece of violence and retribution tonight. He scooped her limp, unconscious body from the back of his sedan and carried her deep within the pitch black, dilapidated facility. He placed her gently onto a stainless-steel table that he had set up in one of the old breakrooms, strapping down her wrists and ankles as he did so. He paused for a moment to admire her young, beautiful face before taping her mouth. He wondered, as he did with all the others before her, how much pain she could endure before mentally breaking. He smiled broadly at the thought, then continued with his setup. He briskly walked back to his car and grabbed two large, black canvas duffels from the back seat. Once back inside, he set up several battery-operated spotlights to illuminate the entire area. The break room was deep inside the building and had no windows, so he didn't fear the lights being seen by any passersby.

She stirred as he arranged his tools on a nearby countertop. He looked back over his shoulder as she began to moan lightly and spoke softly to her in a calming tone. "Easy, little dove. You suffered quite a nasty blow earlier." He walked over to her and reached out his hand to stroke her head. She recoiled violently, eyes wide and full of terror. He reached out with one huge, leathery hand, grabbing her by the throat and squeezing down. "How dare you?! I try to comfort you, and the thanks I get is repulsion?!" She tried once more to scream, but her airway was so constricted that it came out as a mere gurgling sound. He released her, and she began to cough violently and take huge whiffs of air in through her nose. He stood and watched with a maniacal grin as she began to shiver.

"I suppose you have the general questions I always get asked. Who are you? Why are you doing this to me? Why me? Blah, blah, blah. Shortly after I tell you what this is about, you'll try to plead for your life, and I will, of course, ignore you, and then comes the uncontrollable crying and ultimate acceptance of your fate. Finally, the screams will come for the next several hours until you succumb to your injuries and are ultimately purified."

"Let me save you the time and me the trouble, yes? Who I am doesn't matter. I am just a messenger of one greater than myself. What truly matters is who you are, Laura Kelly. You are a 26-year-old mother of two and the wife of Michael Kelly, a local construction foreman. That information, however, is irrelevant to the bigger picture. You are a Sunday school teacher at your beloved St Matthew Presbyterian, as well as a member of the choir and an avid reader of the Word of God." He spat onto the dirty, littered tile floor with the last remark, as if he had swallowed something bitter. He continued. "You are a worshipper of the false God of the Hebrews and gentiles alike, and therefore are an affront to the true master of this world and must be punished and purified of your iniquities."

She began to sob, with tears streaming down her face. The sobs then quickly turned to muffled begging as he approached her, and she began to buck against her restraints. The Russian rolled his eyes and audibly huffed as she tried once again to scream. "I so tire of the cowardice of those who constantly profess the protection of their precious God." He

drew back a meaty, clenched fist and came down
hard. There was a silence-piercing crack as the strike
dislocated and fractured the woman's jaw. She
immediately fainted from the pain. The man reached
behind him and retrieved a bottle of smelling salts.
He waved it under her nose, and she was conscious
once again, but only slightly so.

He walked over to the counter and scanned
his instruments for a moment before settling on a
large hunting knife with a long, silver blade, the blade
serrated near the handle. He made his way over to a
small folding table where a battery powered cassette
player had been placed. He pressed "play" on the
device, and the sounds of Rachmaninoff, Concerto
#2 in C minor began to play. He danced mockingly
back over to the table where the helpless woman lay
defeated and frightened, and leaned down to wave
the blade in her face. He lightly ran it down the
length of her blouse, and then ritualistically clipped
off the buttons one at a time. He laid the sides of the
blouse open, exposing her bare chest and abdomen
to the cool night air. "It's time for our dance to
begin, little dove," he flirted with the woman. He
then pressed the edge of the blade where her collar
bones met in the center of her chest and carefully
sliced a deep cut down to her belly button. The
woman let out a garbled and muffled howl of pain,
which the Russian ignored. He ran the blade over her
chest and abdomen several more times, flaying her

torso open with cuts, which began to stream blood like tiny rivers springing up from nowhere out of her body. He picked up a rag and slowly wiped off the knife before setting it back on the countertop.

"How does it feel knowing your almighty God has forsaken you? Go ahead and cry out. Cry out for your supposed savior to strike me down and make the pain stop." He paused to smirk at the woman. "No? How unsurprising. Do you know how many times I've done this? And do you know how many times your God has intervened? None! God is dead! He is a liar and a false deity!" His breath was heavy with rage, and he watched the woman writhe in pain and try repeatedly to cry out.

The Russian turned again to the counter and selected another tool. He held it up and showed it to her, grinning. It resembled a huge metal claw attached to a pair of brass knuckles, with three very long, sharp tines. "This, little dove, is known as a Spanish Tickler. It's one of my favorite toys. It's been used in the past as an interrogation device, but since you have no information I need, it will be just another aid in your purification process." He suddenly lunged at the woman's left thigh, plunging the tines deep into her leg. He laughed hysterically as his victim groaned in agony, and he began raking the device down the length of her quadricep, pulling up blood, muscle, and sinew in the process. The woman's protests of pain were once again brushed aside. He then pulled the Tickler out and immediately plunged it into her right thigh, repeating the gory attack once again. He pulled out the weapon and threw it to the ground with a satisfied and guttural growl.

Blood gushed from the woman's wounds uncontrollably.

Seeing that the woman was on the brink of death, the Russian sighed, almost in disappointment.

"Well, it appears my master has decided he wants me to send you to him quicker than most of the others. I'm sorry, but it appears our dance has abruptly come to an end, little dove. Give him my warmest regards, yes?" He then reached behind him to the countertop one final time and picked up the sledgehammer. As though playing in time to the madness of the moment, the music in the background reached its crescendo as the blows rained down.

Chapter 4

It was just after midnight, and a dense fog had swarmed the area outside the FBI offices. Buddy sat at his desk, staring intently at the crime-scene photographs. He had lost count of the number of these types of photos he had been forced to study over his career, and yet even now, he wasn't used to it. These, however, were particularly disturbing. When he had first opened the case files of the two victims that Charlie had asked him to confirm, he nearly vomited. He had already set in his mind not to jump to conclusions, but he already knew without a doubt that these homicides were the acts of the same monster that snuffed out the lives of his wife and daughter.

The first set of photos belonged to a young woman named Tiffany Wright. She turned eighteen the same day that she disappeared. Pretty, slender, and athletic, she was not only a captain of her varsity volleyball team at Sacred Heart Catholic High School but also the head cheerleader. She was also intelligent, maintaining an almost-perfect GPA, and an extremely faithful member of the Catholic Church. She was the first of the two victims to be found. An older gentleman was walking his dog one evening near a walking trail in a park when the dog alerted him to something in the bushes. When the man approached the spot, he found the young woman's mangled and broken body. The medical examiner's report had stated that the manner of death was "blunt force trauma in multiple areas of the body, leading to abrupt organ failure from internal bleeding."

The second set of photos belonged to Maria Gonzalez. She was a thirty-nine-year-old widow with three young children. An immigrant from Guadalajara, Mexico, she and her husband had recently become U.S. citizens and were saving to buy their first home. A few months before her abduction, her husband, Miguel, had unfortunately passed away in a car accident involving an impaired driver. She had turned to the church for comfort and help with her children, finding both at St Anne's Catholic, where she had taken over as the organist and pianist. Police found her body only a few days before Charlie had called Buddy. She had died from the same style of blunt force trauma as Tiffany.

As Buddy sat deep in thought, there was a knock at his office door that pulled him from his trance. Mya swung open the door with a grim look on her face. "Bud, we gotta go. KCPD just found another one." The news punched Bud square in the gut, and his eyes immediately glanced back down at the photos. "You gonna make it, partner?" Alvarez asked. Bud steadied himself. "Yeah, Mya, I'm ok. Let's go. I gotta rip off the band aid sometime, right?" Bud grabbed his suit jacket from the back of his desk chair and headed for the door. As he and Mya were walking down the hall, Charlie popped his head out of his office, looking exhausted. From his haggard appearance, he had been at the office all day and into the night, just like Bud and Mya. "Keep me posted, you two, and for God's sake, watch your six."

As they made their way to the parking area, Bud noticed that Mya kept glancing over at him as they walked. "What's on your mind, Alvarez?"

Mya replied, "You sure you're gonna be up for this, Bud? I mean, I'm not trying to say you can't handle a crime scene, but, well fuck, boss, you know what I mean!"

Bud forced a smile. "Mya, I appreciate your concern, but you know as well as I do that once we get there, training will kick in like always, and I'll be fine."

Mya gave him a worried look. "Ok, partner, but I'm gonna be watching you. If at any point you look like you're gonna lose your shit, I'm kicking your ass off the crime scene, and you can go wait in the car."

"Yes, ma'am," Buddy quipped, even though inside he was completely unsure of himself. "Whatever you say, ma'am." At this point, he was trying to put Mya at ease.

"Asshole," Mya shouted as she punched him in the arm. "You make sure to take care of yourself out here, or I'll tell Mom."

"Oh, shit! Don't do that! Camilla will kick my ass," Bud replied in a sarcastic tone.

"Damn right she will," Mya said, "And I'll help her!"

They finally reached the car, argued for a moment over who would drive (Mya, of course, won), then got into the black, government-issued SUV and set off. As they drove, the two sat in an awkward silence for a few minutes, until, at a red light, Mya broke the lull. "I'm glad you're back, partner. Things just haven't been the same around here since you left. I felt sort of, well, lost while you were gone. You know, kind of like..." she paused. "Like a member of my family was gone or something." Her eyes begin to well up. "Bud, I never really got a chance to tell you, what with the investigation, funeral, and all, but I'm so fucking sorry about what happened. Your girls didn't deserve

47

that. No one deserves that, but especially not them. I felt like Lilly was my little sister, or niece, or something. Mom never had any other kids, you know. So when Lilly died, I felt like part of my soul was ripped away. I've talked to Mom about it several times since, but it never gets any easier. She says that faith in God and time will heal your hurt as well as mine, but I can't see it. I'm sorry for getting so emotional, but I want you to know that no matter what happens with this case, you are like family to me and I will do everything in my power to help you bring this prick down." Her expression hardened, and she fell silent, a hint of embarrassment on her face from oversharing. Buddy placed his hand on her shoulder. "It's ok, Mya. Thank you for everything." He then turned and stared out the window, fighting back the tears.

As Mya drove, Bud spoke softly. "So fill me in a little on what you know. Where are we heading?"

"South Blue Valley," Mya said flatly.

"Ah, shit," Bud replied dejectedly, shaking his head, "This is gonna be bad."

South Blue Valley was a notoriously bad area within Kansas City. With a well-above-average crime rate, it was a common occurrence in the area to have reports of gunshots, screams, and other disturbances. Bud couldn't count the times that they had been called out to assist KCPD with homicides and gang-related activities. He was not looking forward to arriving there. Not only was it a dangerous place to be, but the lack of cooperation from potential witnesses made matters even more difficult. As was the case with most high-crime areas, no one wanted to talk due to fear of retaliation from whoever perpetrated a particular crime, especially homicide. This was not going to be an easy investigation, and he knew it.

Mya turned onto a road that led around the forested edge of a large park. It was almost pitch black except for the vehicle's headlights, and the fog was even thicker here than at the FBI office. Bud knew it would be, since just on the other side of the park was the Blue River, which added to the area's humidity and thus increased the risk of fog at night as temperatures dropped. There were also patches of forest within the park, making visibility even more difficult. Mya then made a right turn into the park itself. As she did, she spoke up.

"The crime scene is just up the road a piece in the park itself. Look off to the right and tell me if you can see anything."

Bud scanned ahead of them for a few seconds, then said, "There," pointing to an area with thick tree cover.

Mya slowed the vehicle to a crawl until they could make out the blue and red flashing lights within the trees. She pulled over to the edge of the road and put the car in park. There was a small sign, illuminated by the headlights, that read, "Walking Trail." The pair left the SUV, but not before grabbing a duffel bag from the back with whatever supplies they thought they might need. Mya reached into her pocket and pulled out her cell. She put it on "speaker," and Bud heard the phone ring. A man's voice answered, saying, "Detective Cho."

Mya replied, "Hey, Mike, it's Agent Alvarez. We're here."

"Sure thing, Agent. I'll have one of my guys come up there and walk you down."

A few minutes later, Mya and Bud saw a flashlight swinging back and forth in the distance, coming towards them. A young, slender officer named Pettite walked up and greeted the partners. He led them to the head of the walking trail, making small talk as they went. Bud could tell from the way the kid was talking that it must be his first major crime scene, from the mixture of uneasiness and excitement in his tone. They walked past several officers posted to guard the scene's perimeter, then started down the trail itself. About halfway down, they saw the spotlights and the bright yellow tape that were keeping the scene from being overrun. A short, stout-looking man wearing a tan trench coat stepped under the tape and greeted them.

"Agent Alvarez, it's nice to see you again. I'm sorry it's under such shitty circumstances as usual," the man said half-jokingly.

"Agreed," replied Mya. "Bud, this is Detective Michael Cho of the KCPD," she continued.

"Nice to meet you, Agent Barrett," Cho said brightly. "Mya and I have worked on a couple of cases together before, and she has told me all about you."

Bud forced a polite smile and returned the gesture. "I hope that's a good thing. You never know with Alvarez."

"Dick," Mya quipped quickly at Bud.

"So what do we have?" Bud asked Cho.

"Well, not a lot to go on yet. We've only been processing the scene for a little while now, but we do have a few details." Cho continued, "A couple going out for a late-night stroll came walking down this trail a couple of hours ago and noticed a bad smell coming from a patch of heavy brush just off to the left over there." He pointed. "The man walked over to check it out and found the victim lying completely nude. They called 911 and waited at the trailhead for us to arrive. Once I arrived on scene, a uniformed officer told me they had found a purse beside the victim. It was lying beside her, with some items inside, including her wallet. My initial suspicion is that this wasn't a robbery gone wrong because the victim's wallet still contained money and credit cards. Plus, there are no signs of a struggle and no blood anywhere. Also, the victim looks to have been deceased for a while. There's no way this was a recent crime."

Bud asked,"What prompted you to contact Alvarez?"

"Come over here, and I'll show you," Cho replied.

He led the two agents over to the body, pulled a small flashlight from his inner jacket pocket, and shone it down. He stated plainly, "According to her driver's license, this is twenty-six-year-old Laura Kelly, resident of our fine city." A young woman was lying on her back, with her upper legs shredded as if a rabid grizzly bear had mauled her. Her chest also had several slices and cuts on it that appeared to have been made with a very sharp object. Her appendages from top to bottom were so mashed and mangled that it looked like she had been hit by a semi-truck.

Jagged sections of bone were protruding from her limbs, along with pieces of fat, muscle, and sinew. "This is why I called," Cho said. "I remember Mya telling me that you two worked on the KC Crusher case, and this looked eerily similar to that. Thought we might have a copycat on our hands."

A chill ran down Bud's spine as he looked over the gory scene. Then he noticed it. "Jesus Christ! Where the fuck is her head?!" The top of the woman's neck, where her head should have been, was just as mangled as the rest of her body. There was no clean cut. The head had been unceremoniously removed with great force and in great haste, as there were shredded folds of skin where it had been ripped away. As Bud noticed these things, Detective Cho frowned deeply and slowly inched his flashlight toward a tree directly behind Laura's destroyed body. There, pinned to the tree with what resembled a railroad spike, was the answer to Bud's question. The eyes had been removed and left lying on the ground at the base of the tree. The hair was matted with coagulated blood, and the mouth was gaped open in an eternal scream that appeared to be the last expression the poor, tortured woman would ever make.

Before Bud could stop his legs from moving any closer, he found himself face-to-face with the severed head. As the detective's light remained fixed on the head, Bud noticed something tucked behind the back of the victim's skull. He quickly put on a pair of latex gloves and carefully removed the object. It was a folded piece of notebook paper. With trembling hands, Bud slowly and methodically unfolded it. His vision blurred, and his breathing began to quicken as he stared at the inked text.

The line was short and to the point, and made Bud's blood run cold as he read: "Bog mertv."

Chapter 5

The mist was beginning to rise slowly off the walking trail in the park. The moon and stars were being suffocated in the night sky by thick, ominous clouds, and a slight, cool breeze groped at the tall grass to either side of the gravel pathway. The pungent smell of decaying leaves on the ground assaulted Bud's nose as he slowly walked back to the area where they had found Laura Kelly. He took his time, not even sure what had caused him to make the drive down to South Blue Valley again, especially at night. That was a lie. He knew exactly why he was there. It had been almost two months since the night her mangled, decapitated body had been discovered lying dumped like a piece of refuse that a pedestrian hadn't felt the need to discard properly. Bud was angry and confused; all this senseless violence, and to what end? None of the women who had been so brutally murdered had deserved their fates. As he walked, he kept running the women's names and crime scene photos through his mind. The only common thread was the extremity of their deaths and the fact that all of them were involved with a church in some form or fashion. Was the unsub some religious zealot, or just a psychopath that got his rocks off by preying on the most innocent and vulnerable people he could find? And then there was the note that was found: "Bog mertv," or roughly translated: "God is dead." Bud knew the unsub was clearly mocking them with this blatant middle finger to his victims.

The next morning, after processing the scene, Bud and Mya returned to the office and went straight to Charlie.

Bud told him there was no longer any reason for doubt.

The KC Crusher was back, and his murders were getting more and more violent with each victim. They had all stayed up that day and late into the night, going over every shred of evidence they had. Yet, therein was the problem. There wasn't any evidence other than the twisted and mutilated bodies of those poor women. Whoever this guy was, he was either extremely smart, extremely lucky, or both. He had never left a shred of physical evidence to point the team in any direction, or even make an attempt at putting together a suspect list.

Bud shook his head, still meandering up the path, and knowing that combing over this area again would be a fruitless endeavor. However, he also knew that sitting at home on his ass wasn't going to get them any closer to catching the bastard, either. He finally made it to the spot where they had found her. Flashes of the woman played like clips of a movie in his head: her shredded, grey skin, her pulverized arms and torso, her gore-covered head pinned to the tree with an eternal scream locked on its face. Then other flashes entered his head as well: the trip to her suburban home, ringing the doorbell, the look on her husband Jimmy's face when they told him that his wife had been taken from him and their children. Bud's eyes began to well up with tears as he snapped himself back to the present and the cold, black night in which he found himself. He began to feel like even the trees around him were beginning to close in and laugh at his lack of success on this case. He stood there, staring at the spot on the ground where she had been.

Suddenly, further down the path, he heard a branch snap. Scanning the darkness, he thought he saw a shadow move just off the path a couple of hundred feet from him. It was a tall, black silhouette, and it began heading quickly in the opposite direction towards the river. Bud pulled his flashlight and sidearm and sprinted down the path. As he did, he called out, "You there! FBI! Stop!" The figure continued quickly down the path away from him. Bud noticed that not only was this shadowy figure big, but it was also extremely fast. Bud was no slouch when it came to running, but he was losing ground to this person.

Finally, as Bud rounded a curve in the trail, he could see the opening to the other end of the path that led out of the wooded area and into a clearing just before it reached the bank of the river. He could no longer see the figure, but he knew the person had to be there somewhere. He hadn't lost so much ground that the person would have time to up and vanish. He slowed as he was almost at the end of the path near the clearing, and then came to a dead stop and froze. Stepping from behind a large oak tree was a hulking man in a black trench coat and hat. He could see the man's face. It was blanketed in shadow. He could, however, see the man's eyes. They were red; glowing red. It was impossible. Nobody had glowing red eyes.

As Bud was talking himself back to reality, the figure reached out with a gigantic arm towards the tree he was hiding behind and pulled another figure in close. It was a woman. She struggled against the man, but he was just too strong. She was slight in frame and had no chance against the brute. Bud raised his weapon and pointed it towards the shadow man. "Ok, sir, just take it easy. My name's Agent Bud Barrett, and I'm with the FBI. We can work through whatever this is. Nobody has to get hurt tonight, but I would like you to let that young woman go. That way, you and I can talk this out." The figure just stared back at him with its cold, ungodly red eyes. The woman began to whimper as the figure put its hand around her neck. "Sir, please release the woman. I promise you we can work this out together.

How about you start by telling me your first name?"
Again, the figure made no answer.

The shadowy form then reached behind the tree to the opposite side of him and pulled out yet another figure. This one was much smaller. Bud's heart sank into his feet. It was a child. From the sound of the cries, it was a little girl. Bud's hands began to shake, but he steeled himself and kept his composure. "Sir, please, talk to me. Let those people go." As he took a step to advance on the shadow, Bud finally heard a voice break through the silence, but it wasn't a man's voice. The clouds began to lift, revealing a pale-yellow moon that cast the woman's face for the first time.

"Bud, please help me."

Bud went almost catatonic. "Su...Susan?"

"Bud, for God's sake, please help me! He's going to kill me!"

"Susan, don't worry. Everything's going to be okay."

Another voice broke into the conversation.
"Daddy? Daddy, please help. The big man is hurting me. It hurts. Please make him stop."

Bud dropped his sidearm from his quivering hands.

"Lilly, it's... It's okay, baby. Daddy's here. Daddy will save you."

A deep, guttural laugh pierced the night, causing Bud's blood to freeze in his veins. A thick Russian accent came from the shadow.

"Hello again, Agent Barrett. So, it looks like you find yourself in quite the predicament once more. It seems that this situation has played out once before, and you're just as useless now as you were then."

Bud swallowed hard, caught his breath, and with an edge of desperation to his voice, replied, "Please, whoever you are, don't hurt them."

"Oh, but I already have Agent Barrett. You see, the mind is a very peculiar thing. It can play tricks on even the most intelligent person. For example, right now, your mind is telling you that your wife and daughter are still alive and right in front of you. I assure you, they're not. What's left of their pathetic corpses is slowly rotting away in the cemetery where you left them. You know, after you failed to save them from me? Tell me. What words of comfort did you attempt to give Susan's parents when you broke the news to them that you had exposed them to my wrath and then failed them when they needed you most? Did you tell them what the coroner told you? Did you tell them that I had tortured your little brat of a daughter in front of Susan to break her mentally? In case you're wondering, the last thing your whore wife saw was me snap your little girl's neck before I jammed a blade through Susan's neck."

Bud howled in pain and anger, "You bastard! I'll kill you, so help me God!"

"There it is," the figure sneered in return. "So help me God. It always seems to come back to that, doesn't it, Agent Barrett? Well, I have some bad news for you! Neither God nor anyone else can save this world from me! Just like you couldn't save these two little cunts."

The shadowy figure grabbed Lilly by her hair and lifted her from the ground while Susan screamed. With a strength no man should possess, he hurled the little girl against a nearby tree. The thud was sickening. Lilly's body went limp as it bounced off the ground and went still. The shadow began to laugh maniacally, and in another swift motion, grabbed Susan around her chest, pulled out a long silver blade, and slowly slit her throat from ear to ear. Her eyes widened as the blood spurted from her neck like a geyser. She didn't have time to make a single sound. The red-eyed figure made the cut so deep that he almost decapitated her, which was apparently the plan from the start, as he dropped the knife and twisted her head. An audible pop could be heard as her body fell to the ground. The man stared at the head for a moment before dropping it to the ground.

Bud cried out in anguish, "No! No! Not again!" He picked up his gun from the ground and began firing over and over into the figure. It was no use. His bullets were passing straight through, and the shadow man continued to laugh at him. Bud began to sob uncontrollably and fell to his knees, completely broken. The figure picked up Susan's body, as well as Lilly's, and laid them in front of Bud, who didn't even have the strength to look up at the man. As the man began to walk away, he looked back over his broad shoulder one more time.

"Give it up, Agent Barrett. You couldn't even save your own family. You will never catch me, and many more will die by my hand right under your very nose. If you continue to push me, I will strip you down to a level that not even your God will be able to love." With that, the shadow man faded away, leaving Bud to suffer the fate of his wife and little girl for a second time. As he peered down into his wife's face, she suddenly looked at him with cold, dead eyes.

"Bud, wake up! Bud!" He felt a hand fall onto his shoulder from behind.

Bud shot up in his desk chair, gasping for air and drenched in sweat. He spun around to see Charlie and Mya standing there.

"What the hell are you still doing here?" Charlie asked.

"Yeah, partner. You must have had one hell of a wicked dream. You were jerking in your sleep like you were fighting the devil," Mya added.

Bud looked around, still a little groggy and confused. "I'm pretty sure I was, Mya."

Chapter 6

August 1945

The heels of the lieutenant's boots clacked against the smooth, grey concrete floor as he made his way down the dimly-lit corridor. As he rounded a corner, he could hear a mixture of muffled screams mixed with weeping. He quickened his pace slightly. Reaching the other end of the hallway, he could also hear, mixed in among the obvious sounds of human suffering to which he had grown accustomed, the music of Rachmaninoff streaming from a gramophone machine. He approached the metal door in front of him slowly, straightened his uniform, and steeled himself against the horrors on the other side. Being accustomed to the tortures he had seen over the recent months didn't mean that they bothered him any less. He knocked. A shout came from the other side; the music ceased, and he heard heavy footsteps approaching the door. It swung open, and the hulking man on the other side, who at first adorned a sharp scowl, softened his expression to one of joy. The lieutenant snapped to attention and saluted.

"Ah, Lieutenant Petrov! How are you today, my friend?" the beastly figure said with an obvious mockery in his tone.

"Thank you for asking, Captain. I am well. I come bearing information for you, sir," Petrov replied sheepishly.

Ever since he was assigned to serve under this new captain, he had become increasingly aware that he was neither a man to be trifled with nor one to be admired. He was a monster. He treated the men serving under him with disdain and disregard. He was cruel, power-hungry, and for all intents and purposes, a madman. Yet he commanded absolute obedience and respect; anyone who chose not to comply would end up in an even worse position, treated like one of his "assignments." For some reason, however, Petrov had managed to avoid his ire. The lieutenant supposed that it wasn't because the captain actually liked him, but rather that he loved to mentally disturb and torture him like a bully on a schoolyard playground. Petrov had a weak constitution, and the captain knew it.

"That's fine, Petrov," the senior officer said flatly, as he swiped the papers from the lieutenant's hand. He then flashed the young man a wicked grin. "I'll get to that in a moment, but first, please come in and see my latest projects."

Petrov swallowed hard. He had dreaded that this might happen, but knew he was powerless to refuse. He stepped inside the room. The lower-ranking soldier gasped at what he saw. Lying on a cold metal table was a woman. She was completely nude and covered in small nicks that appeared to have been created by a knife or other sharp instrument. Blood slowly seeped from each laceration. There were also bruises of different sizes and colors covering the poor thing from head to toe. Some were a deep purple or black, while others had a yellowish tint. Her breathing was shallow, and she looked to have been on the metal slab for a long time. With what breath she could manage, she was letting out soft sobs through a cloth gag in her mouth. She was clearly in an unbearable amount of pain, as her eyes rolled around in their sockets randomly and her eyelids drooped from fatigue.

As Petrov tried in vain to gather his wits at this sight, he heard a sharp cry come from a corner of the room. A young man was bound to a chair with his arms behind him and his ankles tied to the legs. He tried to cry out in a full-throated protest against what was happening, but something blocked his voice. It was then that the lieutenant realized the cause of the man's distress. He took a few steps closer to confirm what his eyes were telling him. He immediately stepped back in horror. The man opened his mouth to cry out again, and Petrov could see that his tongue had been removed. Noticing the man's other injuries only heightened Petrov's disgust and shock. The man was covered in bruises and cuts just like the woman, but worst of all, his eyelids had been cut away, revealing almost the entirety of the eyes themselves. Petrov began to shake involuntarily, but then quickly gathered himself, knowing that if the captain noticed, he would be in for harsh punishment. The captain detested any signs of weakness.

"Captain, might I inquire as to what all of this is about?" the lieutenant asked in the most respectful tone he could muster.

The captain smiled. "Of course, my friend! Do you enjoy seeing my work?" He pointed to the man in the corner. "This is Private Sergei Popov. He is a deserter, and therefore a treasonous coward to our cause. He was deemed guilty in court after some of his fellow soldiers testified that he became frightened and attempted to run in one particular fire exchange with the enemy. He was sentenced to hang, but I convinced the judge to allow me to use him as an example for a time to educate newly enlisted men on the perils of desertion during wartime. Make no mistake. He will hang for his crime, but not before his greater purpose has been served. The woman you see on the table is his wife, Katerina. She is guilty of no actual crime, of course, except for being married to a lesser man. However, her own purpose is to drive home further the point I want to make to the others. There is no room for fear in this military, and any man showing fear will pay dearly. That all being said, I will torture and kill the private's wife in front of him, and then once he is brought to the brink of absolute madness, onto my table he will go to suffer the most horrible death I can imagine for him."

At these words, Katerina began to weep. Petrov was paralyzed in hidden terror as the captain walked over the woman and punched her hard in the face. There was an audible crack that echoed through the room as her cheekbone crumbled like clay under the captain's powerful blow. Blood spurted from her nose and mouth. Gurgled cries came from the man in the corner as he watched his wife be assaulted right in front of him. The captain quickly walked over to the gramophone and turned the music back on. He grabbed a container of salt, walked over to the woman, and in measured tones, said, "I will now salt this field to ensure that the seeds of discord will not grow." He began smashing handfuls of salt into the cuts that covered the woman, and she began to moan and wail as loudly as her exhausted body would allow.

The man in the corner, with no other recourse, began smashing his head into the wall behind him in an attempt to knock himself unconscious so he would no longer have to watch his wife suffer such violence. Looking over at the private, the captain looked back at Petrov and sneered. "Lieutenant, go over there and take hold of the coward's head. Make him watch the suffering he has caused by his own actions. You hold him still. Go!" Petrov reluctantly did as he was told, walking over to the man and grabbing two handfuls of his hair, holding his head still. The captain laughed as he jammed another wad of salt into a particularly nasty cut on the young woman's leg. He then walked back over to the table and set down the salt.

He picked up the papers that Petrov had brought to him. His face brightened once again in a manner that concerned the lieutenant more than put him at ease. He sat them back down and walked to the far edge of the table. Petrov could only watch as his captain picked up an object and admired it. He showed it to the lieutenant. "Do you know what this is, Petrov? This is called a Spanish Tickler. It has been used in the past as a highly effective interrogation tool. Even though there is no actual questioning to be done here, its uses are still effective for my own projects." Petrov shuddered at this last statement. The metal claw was extremely ominous and intimidating just on the face of it. He didn't even want to imagine the "uses" to which the captain was referring.

"But it appears that the rest of this particular cleansing session will have to wait." Petrov's relief at this news was only short-lived. His stomach went into his feet at the captain's next proclamation. "The news you brought to me is joyous indeed! It seems that I have direct orders to meet personally with Secretary General Stalin immediately. What an honor this will be!" He clapped his hands together loudly. "Come, lieutenant, escort me out! I believe great things may be in store for me sooner rather than later!" Petrov paused. "Sir, what about the, uh, prisoners?"

"Oh, that's right," he sneered. The captain handed the Spanish Tickler to Petrov and led him over to Katerina. "We can't leave yet; not when there's still work to be done.

Petrov began to shake as the realization set in as to what was about to happen. "There's no time like the present, my friend, to start learning!" Petrov said, amused. "Now, take the tickler and jam it into the bitch's stomach." Petrov slowly began shaking his head. "Lieutenant, I gave you an order," the captain said sharply. Again, the young man shook his head as he began to shake. Suddenly, the bigger man grabbed Petrov's wrist and thrust it downward. The lieutenant nearly wretched as he felt the tines of the tickler slide effortlessly and deeply into the woman's torso. She started to scream, but the pain was too much, and she passed out almost immediately. In the corner, her husband howled with a mixture of pain and hatred. The captain cheered with delight and let go of his lesser' s wrist. He took back the tool. "Well, it appears you're not quite ready to take up my mantle just yet, Petrov, but you will be. Petrov immediately understood that this was a test, and he had failed it miserably. Worst of all, he now had to live with the fact that it was his hand that dealt this poor woman the killing blow, not the captain. The man in the corner continued to struggle and sob.

"Well, then, lieutenant, I must be off. I need to prepare for my trip to see our glorious leader. Obviously, I can't leave these two to their own devices, so you are ordered to stay here with them until I send someone to relieve you. Perhaps some time with your handywork will allow you to reflect on the importance of loyalty within your own actions." The captain's words were dripping with disdain, and Petrov knew that staying here to watch the woman slowly bleed out was his punishment for hesitating to do as his superior requested. As the captain walked away, the young lieutenant felt his own guts tighten, and a wave of nausea caused him to vomit on his own boots.

The next day, the captain stood smugly outside the

Secretary General's door. He had waited for this moment for a very long time. He greatly admired Secretary General Stalin, even though he disagreed with the unnecessary use of diplomacy his leader had recently employed in talks with their enemies. The captain prided himself on being a man of action. Words paled in comparison to the use of direct force to accomplish a goal. Nonetheless, his heart pounded in his chest as he stood waiting. He didn't have to wait long, as at that moment, the office door slowly opened. A lower-ranking soldier led him in, saluted, and then left the room, closing the door behind him. The captain was surprised to find no other high-ranking officials in the room. There was only him and Stalin. Shaking off the thought, he stood at attention and saluted.

"No need for all of the formalities, Captain," Stalin said evenly. "Please, have a seat, and we'll get started."

"Thank you, sir," the captain replied. He sat down in a large leather chair across from Stalin's desk.

The Secretary General began. "The reason I requested your presence, Captain, is that some information has come to me that needs to be addressed immediately. I have asked around and have been told by many that you and your particular skill set are just what I need to handle a sensitive and very important situation. As you may know, I recently met with President Truman of the United States and Prime Minister Churchill of Britain. Needless to say, the meeting did not go well, and I fear it was not in our favor either. They were hesitant at best to hear out our side of things." Stalin exhaled loudly. "Captain, this concerns me greatly, and quite frankly, it cannot stand. That, my friend, is where you come into play. I have heard of your tactics being, shall we say, direct and unorthodox. However, that is exactly the type of tactics I need right now." His gaze became sterner.

"Captain, what I am about to tell you next cannot leave this room. You and I are the only two souls who will ever know this plan. If you divulge any of this information, you will go straight in front of a firing squad for treason. There will be no trial. Is that understood?"

The captain replied, "Yes, sir. I would never betray your trust."

"Good," Stalin replied. "With the lack of cooperation from the US and Britain, I feel that we may not be long off from another war between the three of our countries. I intend to avoid this by strong-arming Truman and Churchill into surrendering before it ever comes to that. They cannot be allowed to dictate to us how we proceed with our own country's affairs."

The captain nodded attentively. "With all due respect, sir, these countries are extremely powerful; possibly just as powerful as we are. How do you expect to have them bend the knee without a major conflict?"

"As you know," Stalin resumed, "Adolf was a man who was rumored to believe deeply in the occult. He had many artifacts that supposedly held different levels of significance within the same. I also believe in such things, Captain, and there is one particular item in his collection that I would like to retrieve. It is said to be an item that holds within it the power to bring down the entirety of humanity in the proper hands. It is a talisman said to contain unimaginable power. According to my history experts, this talisman contains the essence of Lucifer himself, and if it works as the rumors say, I will use it to bend the allied countries to my will. I need you to retrieve it for me by any means necessary. The rewards you receive for this service will be beyond count, my friend."

"Where do I find this talisman, sir, and what does it look like?"

Stalin continued, "The talisman is a vial of red glass in the shape of a human heart. It is surrounded by veins of gold that lead to a center figure of a ram with a star inlaid in its forehead. The vial is suspended from a braided gold chain. As to its whereabouts, that is the part that will cause the most difficulty. According to intelligence, after its previous owner ended his life, it was stolen from his collection, possibly by a group of American soldiers who took it back to their country with them as spoils of war. You must locate this item no matter the cost. You will, of course, have all the resources that you need to acquire it. The full weight of my office is at your disposal, Captain. Do not let me down."

The captain once again donned his sinister grin. "Sir, while I do not personally believe in the occult, magic, or even heaven or hell, I do believe in your leadership and the privilege of serving my country. If the talisman is important to you, I will see this task done, General Stalin."

"Good man," Stalin grinned. "Now tell me what you need."

Chapter 7

Bud awoke with a start; his head still swimming. He groggily looked around his studio apartment. "What the fuck?" he wondered to himself. "What time is it? Hell, for that matter, what day is it? Man, I must have really tied one on last night." He sat up, rubbing his temples. His head was pounding like someone was taking a jackhammer to it. He hadn't been this hungover in a long time; not since, well, not since the day after the funerals. He peered out of the big bay windows. The sky was pitch black. He was thankful for the darkness. At least it wasn't daylight outside. That would really have done a number on his already aching brain. "Sunday," he muttered to himself. "It's Sunday morning. It must be." He was beginning to remember the events of the previous night.

He had ended his workday on Friday around three o'clock and told Charlie and Mya that he wouldn't be back in until Monday morning unless something major happened. He fully intended to take advantage of a couple of days to himself. He badly needed a reset. Between the sixteenhour workdays and the nightmares he had been having, his brain was completely fried. He needed to take his mind off things for a bit and unwind. He went home Friday night and tried to get some rest after an early dinner, but the nightmares returned, and he couldn't doze off at all. Saturday morning began as a continuation of Friday night, as he lay there staring at the ceiling with bloodshot eyes. He got up and forced himself to go to the gym, thinking that maybe he could physically wear himself out enough to go home and pass out from exhaustion. That didn't happen, either. Finally, around 8 pm, he found himself wandering the Kansas City streets until he wound up in front of the one place he really shouldn't be. He stared up at the blinking neon sign: "Beau's Place, Beau's Place, Beau's Place," it beckoned to him. Bud opened the door and walked in somewhat hesitantly, but not really; not if he was really being honest with himself.

Now, here he was, his head on fire and his stomach churning. "Fuck," he mumbled aloud. "I was doing well there for a bit. Can't believe I let it happen again. Oh well, I can't change it now. I gotta try even harder to square my ass away." Bud picked up his phone and pushed the power button on the side. The screen flashed on, and the digital clock read "Sunday, October 17, 10:37 pm." He slowly shook his head, believing his hungover eyes might be deceiving him.

He clicked the button and checked his phone again. To his dismay, the time remained the same.

"You gotta be fucking kidding me! I slept an entire fucking day! Goddamn it!" That's when he noticed it. He was so distracted by the fact that he had somehow wasted a whole day getting plastered at Beau's that he nearly missed the voicemail icon at the top of the screen. Now he was even more angry at himself. Had he gotten so blackout drunk that he missed some important phone call? He unlocked his phone and opened his call log. The last incoming call attempt was from Mya nearly two hours ago. Moreover, the last *four* missed calls were from Mya. Bud's stomach dropped into his feet. She and Charlie were gonna be so pissed at him. He smacked himself in the forehead. "Fucking asshole!" He then clicked the voicemail icon and put the phone to his ear.

The robotic voice chimed into existence. "Please enter your passcode." He punched in six, nine, six, nine. It was a dirty joke between him and Susan. She had called him a "Freaking perv" when he told her it was the easiest number for him to remember. Bud almost involuntarily cracked a smile, but then quickly snapped back.

"You have four new messages," the feminine voice rhythmically stated. "First message..."

Mya's voice started. "Hey, Boss. It's Alvarez. Sorry to bother you, but KCPD just received an anonymous tip about a suspicious-looking person near St Joe's Catholic on the west side of town. Apparently, it's an old, abandoned church that hasn't been used in a few years. Charlie and I are gonna head over and meet up with Detective Cho and some blues to check it out. Thought you should know and maybe get down here, too. Sounds like this may be a credible lead, based on Cho's comments. Call me back when you get this."

"Message received on Sunday, October 17th at 8:45 pm. Next message..."

"Hey, Boss. Haven't heard from you yet. Thought I'd try again. We're on scene just a few blocks away, and Cho is getting ready to brief us on the situation. Call me."

"Message received on Sunday, October 17th at 9:15 pm. Next message..."

"Boss, why the hell aren't you answering your phone. We're just a couple of minutes from breaching the building. One of the officers scouting the building radioed that he might have seen movement inside. Please hurry up and fucking call me!"

"Message received on Sunday, October 17th at 9:30 pm. Next message..."

Mya's voice was a panicked, gurgling whisper. "Bud..."

"Message received on Sunday, October 17th at 10:30 pm. End of messages."

Bud's ears began to ring with a high-pitched whining noise, and a lump formed in his throat. He involuntarily dropped his phone on the bed. He heard himself say in a shaky voice, "Oh, my God! Mya. Charlie." Then he heard another, louder voice yell, "Get up, you fucking idiot! Move!" He jumped to his feet, throwing on his clothes as quickly as he could. Grabbing his gear and car keys, he rushed out the door, not even bothering to lock it behind him. A few seconds later, which felt like an eternity to him at that point, Bud was in his car, slapping his magnetic red flashing light to the roof and starting the engine. It roared to life, and he slapped the shifter into drive and stomped the gas pedal. He sped down the street in front of his complex and grabbed his phone from the passenger seat. Calling Detective Cho's office, he reached the desk sergeant and got the church's address. He quickly hung up, punched the address into his car's GPS, and sped into the night.

As Bud drove on, passing cars with reckless abandon, swerving to the left, to the right, and then left again, he began to play out every awful scenario in his mind. What had happened? Was he there? Was it someone else? Had they stumbled onto some gang-affiliated activity? Was there a shootout? Was Mya or Charlie hurt, or did they make it out okay? Mya certainly didn't sound okay, and that made Bud sick to his stomach. If anything were to happen to her or Charlie, he would never forgive himself, never, especially after he had spent the previous night being a drunk asshole.

He could see the red and blue flashing lights from several blocks away, and Bud's vision began to tunnel. The entire area was lit up with first-responder vehicles of every kind: police cruisers, ambulances, fire trucks, and even FBI. Then, his heart almost stopped. As he got closer, he saw what he feared the most and had hoped wouldn't be there: forensics vehicles and a coroner's van. Bud brought his car to a sudden halt, still several hundred feet away from the scene. He threw it in park and just sat there staring at the intimidating gothic structure. It was still mostly intact, even though it hadn't been used in quite a while. Its gargoyles were perched high above on the ledges, peering down at him almost mockingly as if to say what he already knew, "You're too late."

Bud stepped out of his car as if on autopilot. His arms and legs were moving, but somehow he didn't feel like he was in control of them. He watched himself from a distance as his body weaved through the swarm of officers, reporters, and onlookers. Just as he was about to cross the police tape, someone grabbed his shoulder hard, and he snapped back into himself.

"Sir," a young, but very fit, uniformed officer scolded, "I can't let you past the line. This is a crime scene."

Bud looked at the officer blankly for a moment, blinked himself back to reality, and showed the man his badge. "FBI," Bud heard himself say, still not sure of what the hell he was doing or how he had even gotten this far.

The young officer held up his index finger as if to say, "Hang on a second." He then grabbed the radio clipped to his shirt and said something into it. Bud couldn't quite make it out because his hearing had become muffled, like he was listening to someone speak while underwater. The officer spoke into the radio once more, then looked at Bud. "Hang on just a second, Agent Barrett. One of your colleagues is coming out to meet you."

Bud nodded slowly and stood there, numb from head to toe. A couple of minutes later, a tall, well-muscled man in a black suit exited the church doors and walked over to Bud. He had a look of despair and sickness on his face so severe that Bud had only seen its like one other time: while he looked in the bathroom mirror at the office the night his wife and daughter were slaughtered. "Hey, Bud," the man said slowly and hesitantly.

Bud looked up at the man and, seeing him standing there, was temporarily brought back to life. "Tommy?" Bud asked. He had only met Agent Bruski a couple of times, but he seemed like a good person and a good agent. The young man seemed to love his job and take it seriously.

"Bud, I know what you're thinking, and you really don't want to go in there."

"What the fuck happened, Tommy?" Bud demanded.

"It's bad, Bud," Tommy replied solemnly. "It's a massacre. Twelve uniformed officers and Detective Cho are dead and..." He trailed off.

"And what, Tommy?"

Tommy's bottom lip began to quiver, but he steeled himself. "And two agents."

"Mya and Charlie?" Bud asked sheepishly, sorrowfully.

"Yeah," Tommy responded. "Jesus. I'm so sorry, Bud." The big kid placed his hand on Bud's shoulder and lightly squeezed.

Bud went silent for several moments, staring intently at the pavement. He then looked up at Agent Bruski with a determined, even somewhat angry look and stated, "Tommy, take me in there. I need to see. Don't try to stop me. Please do as I ask." Tommy just nodded back and held the tape up for Bud to walk underneath. Then they both walked slowly towards the cathedral doors and stepped inside.

On the other side of the doorway, Bud stopped and immediately had to run back outside to wretch. Tommy ran after him, asking him if he was okay. The initial shock of what he saw was too much to bear. He vomited to the point where he began to dry-heave. Wiping his mouth, he looked back over his shoulder at Tommy.

"Jesus! Fuck! Tommy, how the fuck could this happen?!"

Tommy looked down, like a dog being scolded after nosing through the trash. Sheepishly, he replied, "I tried to tell you that you didn't want to see it, Bud. I'm sorry."

Bud felt a little guilty about chewing the kid. He took a deep breath through his nose to calm himself. "I'm sorry, Tom. I didn't mean to snap. It just doesn't make sense. How could one person move fast enough to take down fifteen-armed law enforcement agents? There had to be more than one person in on this. Either that, or there had to be some trap laid; some sort of ambush, you know?" Tommy just shook his head. "We're all dumbfounded, Agent Barrett. Everybody working the scene is giving it everything they've got on this one."'

Bud placed his hand on Bruski's shoulder. "Speaking of, let's head back in now."

"Are you sure, Bud?" Tommy asked, a little shocked.

"We're not doing those victims any good by just sitting out here getting sick, Tommy. Let's go get to work so we can catch whoever did this and give them peace, yeah?" Bud was putting on his bravest face for Tommy to put him at ease. Truth be told, however, Bud was scared shitless and wanted nothing more than to turn and bolt. No part of him wanted to go back into that disaster area, nor to see his friends in such a state. Yet, that annoying voice that had driven Bud to leave his apartment was now back and hounding him again. The marine in him said loudly, "Honor them, Bud. Honor your fallen brother and sister. Get your ass in there and figure this shit out." Once he regained control of himself, he stepped back inside the church. Walking forward slowly with Tommy in tow, his heart began pounding so loudly that he could feel it in his ears. His breathing also reached a fever-pitch, as he almost started to hyperventilate.

He steadied himself and took in the gruesome scene. Blood was spattered and sprayed across nearly every surface in the large auditorium. The iron-laden odor was almost enough to make Bud need another trip outside, but he remained, transfixed by the sight. Behind the pulpit, two long folding tables, like the kind churches use for gatherings, were set side by side and draped with a tablecloth. The stark contrast between the snow-white fabric and crimson smears was unsettling to say the least.

Set at the very center of the table was a robed figure, his hands out to his sides in a welcoming gesture. Bud recognized the man immediately. It was Detective Cho's body, dressed to look like Jesus Christ. The poor bastard had been tied to the podium so that his body would remain upright, and he had been disemboweled; his intestines spread out onto the table before him. To either side of him, six mutilated corpses sat at the table in different poses. Numbering twelve in total and barely recognizable from the injuries they sustained, Bud knew these were the KCPD officers who had accompanied the detective. On the tabletop, the officers' hands, feet, ears, and other body parts were splayed out, forming a macabre feast. It came to Bud instantly. This was a clear mockery of The Last Supper.

Bud felt a surge of electricity shoot down his spine. At the same time, he felt himself begin to shake uncontrollably. He tried his best to stem the tide of emotions running through him, and it was hard, but he managed it. That was, until he looked over to a small area behind the pulpit. There, in the baptismal, in a makeshift manger scene, were Mya and Charlie. They had also been placed in costume robes and then posed kneeling. They appeared to be holding something, but Bud couldn't quite make it out, so he walked closer. Examining the bodies closer, Bud found it odd that they had no immediate signs of trauma, that is, until he removed the cloth from their heads, revealing that both their necks had been broken. The attacker clearly wanted them intact for this staging. From their angle, it looked like they were sharing the burden of holding something in a blanket. As Bud was about to remove the soft fleece throw, his phone buzzed with a text message. He opened it to see that the message was from Mya's phone. It read, "Unto us this day is born a savior, but not yours, Agent Barrett. This is your last warning to let this go, or the next crime scene to be examined will be your own. Do svidaniya."

Bud's hands began to shake violently as he dropped his phone for the second time in a matter of hours. He reached out to remove the blanket, and as it slid away, his deafening screams echoed through the vaulted ceilings of the church. As his brain tried in vain to process the sight of the decapitated newborn in front of him, darkness took him, and he dropped to the floor with a thud.

Chapter 8

The sky was draped with rain clouds, as if it were night. The funeral had ended an hour ago, but Bud stood at the freshly dug grave, soaked to the bone. His overcoat and umbrella did little to keep out the misty water droplets, nor did they keep out the cold that was chilling his bones. He suspected that the latter had less to do with the environment and more to do with the feelings of sorrow and dread deep in the pit of his stomach. He had cried so much over the past little while that he had worn himself to the point of exhaustion. He just stood over Mya, muttering the words "I'm sorry" over and over at an inaudible volume. He had done the same at Charlie's funeral not two days ago, and at the funeral for little Maddy Monroe, the six-month-old he found with Mya and Charlie, a day before that. It wasn't any easier then than now.

Trapped deep in his own mind and completely numb to the world around him, he kept replaying the events of the prior week over and over again. What the hell had happened? Why the fuck had he drunk so much? What in the world possessed him to even drink in the first place? Why hadn't Beau cut him off? Why the fuck didn't he wake up and answer Mya's calls? What if he had? Would he have gone down there and died, too? How the fuck did one person ambush fifteen people and brutally murder them without them getting off a single shot at him? The higher-ups asked the same questions about the murder investigation that followed, but came up with the same answer as Bud: no answer at all. Not a lick of forensic evidence or hypothetical detective work turned up a shred of a theory. They were all completely perplexed. None of this made sense. It was all a blur; a horrible fucking nightmare from which there was no waking.

As he stood there in his zombified state, he almost didn't feel the light touch of a hand on his forearm. He did, though, and the shock of it almost made him lose his balance and fall into the hole where his partner and friend was currently lying. "Shit!" he yelped. He whipped around, fully intending to give the person a piece of his mind for startling him, until he saw who it was. In front of him stood Camilla Alvarez, Mya's mother. Her black dress gently flowed in the breeze, and her umbrella swayed from a combination of the wind and her lack of strength to hold it steady. Her brown eyes looked at him knowingly, softly, and she wore a very slight, empathetic smile.

"Hola, Bud," she said to him in a whisper-like tone.

"Hi, Camilla," Bud sheepishly replied. His eyes quickly went to the ground to avoid looking at her for fear of crying again.

"Mijo, what are you still doing here? I didn't see you at the reception and got worried. You're soaked and will catch your death out here."

Bud felt an awkwardness to that last phrase. He didn't know whether to laugh at it or cry. "I'm sorry, Camilla. I didn't mean to worry you. It's just, well, I don't really feel like being around people right now, and I didn't want Mya to be alone out here."

The petite woman placed a hand on Bud's shoulder and let out a shaky sigh. "Oh, Mijo. My Mya isn't here. She's in the arms of the Lord now. Nothing or no one can harm her, and she is the happiest she's ever been; happier than we are here."

Bud felt a twinge of anger rise in his gut, but then quickly pushed it back down. He thought to himself, "Knock your shit off, dumbass. Camilla is showing concern for you when she has just lost her daughter. Act like you've got some sense and thank her." Instead, all that came out of him was, "Camilla, I admire your faith, but I don't know if I can believe that anymore. I'm not even sure I believe that there's a heaven or even if God himself exists anymore. If God exists, why would he let something like this happen to someone as wonderful as Mya, or Charlie, or anyone for that matter?"

"Bud, Mijo, God didn't allow this to happen. All of the evil, wicked things that happen in this world are the work of the devil alone. God does not intervene because he has his own reasons and plans for us. It is not our right to question that. For God to interfere with the actions of man would be for him to interfere with the free will that he gave each of us in the first place. Good or bad, men will do as they please, and each of us will reap what we sow in the next life, even if justice is never served to us here. Mya understood that, just as she understood the risks of being an FBI agent. She loved what she did, just as she loved you and Charlie."

At that last statement, Bud couldn't hold it back anymore. He hung his head and began to sob heavily. "Camilla, I'm so sorry. I'm sorry I wasn't there to protect your daughter. I'm sorry I wasn't there to protect Charlie. I'm sorry for everything."

Camilla gave him a stern look. "Mijo, enough of this talk!

Do you understand me?!" She reached up and lifted Bud's chin. "This is a time to honor my daughter's sacrifice, not wallow in self-pity. Come. Let's go back to the house and finish our conversation out of the storm."

Even in that moment of absolute
hopelessness, Bud couldn't help but admire Camilla's
strength and resolve. A level to which he would
probably never ascend. As he looked at her
determined eyes, all he could muster was a weak,
"Yes, ma'am."

After reaching the Alvarez home, Camilla
sent Bud into the bathroom to dry off and change.
Her husband was slightly smaller than he was, so the
clothes she gave him were a little ill-fitting. However,
he put them on anyway, so as not to offend the fiery
Hispanic woman a second time. He stepped out of
the bathroom, still running the damp towel through
his salt-and-pepper hair. He looked around to see the
rest of the home empty; only ten minutes earlier,
there had been several people there.

Bud looked at Camilla and her husband,
Manuel, with confusion. "Where did everybody get
off to so quickly?" he asked.

"I sent them home. I needed to have some
peace and quiet to speak with you, and my relatives
have no idea how to provide either of those things,"
Camilla said flatly.

Bud was once again reminded of where Mya
got her spirited personality from, and he couldn't
help but grin slightly. He could also tell that Manuel,
who was a quiet man to begin with, felt like a third

wheel standing there, so he welcomed Bud but then quickly excused himself to another room.

"Come with me, Mijo," Camilla said as she motioned for Bud to follow her down the hallway just off the kitchen.

They walked past a small bathroom on the left and a bedroom on the right. They stopped at a closed door at the end of the hall. Camilla placed her hand on the doorknob, hesitated for a moment, let out a deep breath, and then pushed the door open gently. She looked to her immediate left and flipped on a light switch. She motioned for Bud to come into the room.

"This was Mya's room. She had her own place, obviously, but sometimes she stayed here with us on weekends. Did you know that?"

Bud shrugged slightly. "No, I didn't."

Looking around the room, Bud could see little bits of Mya everywhere. There was a solid oak dresser and a chest of drawers littered with hairbands, brushes, makeup kits, and other hygiene items. Stuffed animals covered what Bud could only assume was a bed, because there were so many that you could barely see the white comforter underneath. Mya had a strange obsession with Hello Kitty, and there were about ten different characters from that universe currently adorning the queen-sized mattress. He remembered all the times that he had ribbed her over collecting such memorabilia, asking her, "What are you, like twelve or something?"

He also noticed a small end table next to the bed with what Bud assumed was a makeshift prayer area: a candle in a long glass container bearing a picture of the Virgin Mary. There was also a rosary lying there, along with a few other religious items. Watching Bud look over the table, Camilla walked over to the dresser and opened a small wooden jewelry box. Bud shifted to one side to try to look over her shoulder. It wasn't necessary, though, because she turned to him, holding a necklace in her hand. She let it drop, allowing the chain to dangle from her fingers. At the end of the chain was a small pendant, and Camilla held it up to show him.

"Do you know what this is?" she asked him.

"It looks like a catholic protection pendant. Maybe a saint?" Bud replied hesitantly. He was a little rusty with his catholic traditions. He hadn't been to church since he had gone with his wife and daughter.

"That's right, Mijo. This," she held up the pendant, "is St. Jude. He is the patron saint of lost causes." She walked over to Bud with her hand outstretched. "Mya had recently gotten this necklace for you. She said it was a mixture of a joke and a gift of deep appreciation and love for you, Bud. She adored you and looked up to you, you know." She attempted to place the necklace in his hand.

Bud raised his hands slowly, not in a defensive way, but rather to say, "Sorry, Camilla, but I can't accept this. I don't deserve it."

Camilla gently grabbed Bud's right hand and pressed the pendant into it. "Bud, Mya bought this specifically for you. She even went down to our church and had Father Bradley bless it for you. Please, take it. I know she would have been smiling from ear to ear if she could have given it to you herself."

A sudden strong wave of grief and sorrow caused Bud's knees to become weak, and he had to walk over and sit down on the edge of Mya's bed for a moment to gather himself. Camilla could see the rush of emotion take him, so she sat down and took his hands in hers once more. She then looked him thoughtfully and deeply in his eyes, and spoke.

"Bud, I know you blame yourself for what happened to Mya and Charlie, but this isn't your fault. This was the act of a deranged and heartless man. As I said earlier, Mya knew the risks involved with her job. She loved being an agent anyway, and she loved working with you and Charlie even more. You were like the older brothers she never had. She spoke often of you and how much she admired your grit and determination. She was devastated for you when you lost your girls. She prayed for you constantly, and that's what led her to give you this necklace. She felt that the protection of St Jude would help you through all of this mess; that it would keep you safe and levelheaded in times of hopelessness and great need. Bud, I need you to promise me that you'll wear this necklace in her memory, not for me, but for what *you* meant to her and how much she believed in you. I know your faith in God is wavering right now, but I can assure you that his faith in you will never waver. She would want you to keep going, not shut down or give up. I didn't know Charlie as well as I know you, but I'm sure he would feel the same way. God has set this obstacle in your path for a reason. It's up to you to figure out what that reason is and what you can do to overcome it. Do you understand, Mijo?"

Bud sat silently for a few moments, deep in his own thoughts. Then he gently squeezed Camilla's hands and said, "Camilla, I don't know how I'll make it through all of this, or even if I *will* make it through this, but I promise you that I will try my best for Mya and Charlie. Your daughter was the best of the three of us by a long shot, and I will do everything in my power to honor her memory and sacrifice for the rest of my life." With that, he stood up, placed the pendant around his neck, and wrapped his late partner's mother in a long, warm embrace. They cried and laughed together well into the night.

Chapter 9

Sitting in the breakroom of the abandoned building where he performed his works of art, the Russian sat with a half drunk bottle of vodka on the small stainless-steel table in front of him. Seemingly coming from the void of the darkness behind him, a composition from Sergei Prokofiev was softly manifesting itself into his ears. He swayed gently to the rhythm, almost forgetting himself and his current task. Coming to his senses, he reached behind him into the inner pocket of the black trench coat flung over the back of the chair in which he was sitting. Opening the cell phone's lock screen, he found the wallpaper filling his vision. The beautiful Hispanic agent stood with someone he assumed was her mother, smiling widely, eyes bright. They stood before a brightly colored carousel of shining plastic horses, each woman holding a bright pink tuft of cotton candy on a white cardboard cone. It was a sweet scene, he thought to himself briefly.

Then he remembered how much sweeter the scene had been when he had left her just a few nights earlier. He had found it quite satisfying to throttle the bitch after finding the rosary in her jacket pocket; another follower of the false god. He had squeezed her neck until it popped like a champagne cork, and then he had displayed her and her bothersome partner for Agent Barrett to find so that the bothersome asshole's mind was broken beyond repair. He could leave it at that, but instead, he had decided that the agent had been a thorn in his side for far too long, not that he had ever come anywhere near to catching him, or even that it would matter if it did. The moment Agent Barrett even came within eyeshot, he would end him like all the others that had come before him over the decades past. This, however, would have to wait a while longer. He had set his mind to drag this out and make Barrett's mental pain last far longer than the physical pain he would inflict later.

Grinning to himself at the thought of adding the agent to his tally, he pressed the little green phone icon and punched in the number from the card in his other hand. It rang three times, and then a man with a gruff, yet high pitched voice said flatly, "Donovan." "Do it," the Russian said in his thick accent.

"On it," the man replied.

Chapter 10

Lenny sat at his cluttered desk, staring off into space as usual. "Fuck!" he hissed under his breath as the blob of raspberry jelly from his fourth donut of the morning plopped onto his tie. "I just got this fucking tie!" he yelled at himself again. He reached to open the top desk drawer to his right, but because he was so angry with himself for ruining his thrift store tie, he pulled too hard and ripped the drawer all the way out and dumped its contents onto the floor. "You gotta be shitting me!" he exclaimed as he rolled his eyes. He spun his rolling desk chair to the side, and as he did, the chair moaned and creaked in protest because of the large man's girth. His breathing came in short, ragged bursts as he bent over to pick up the plastic flatware, napkins, sugar packets, wet naps, mint-flavored toothpicks, and other eating utensils.

"Jesus Christ, Horowitz," someone said behind him. Lenny could tell right away that it was Gavin. It was *always* Gavin. That little prick had seemingly made it his personal mission to aggravate him every chance he got. He thought he was such a hot little shit and better than Lenny just because he was the main investigative reporter for the Kansas

City Inquisitor, and Lenny was just a low-level beat writer. It made Lenny want to clock him in his smug little face.

"Eat my dick, Hansen," Lenny retorted.

"Get me a forklift to pick up your gut, and I will, you fat fuck," Gavin chuckled as he walked away from Lenny's desk.

Lenny just flipped him the bird and continued to pick up his sundries, panting like a male dog in heat. Lenny hated being fat. Lenny hated pretty much every aspect of his life. He hated his shitty job, his shitty editor, all of his shitty coworkers, his shitty apartment, and his shitty car.

He once had a very promising journalism career in his younger days, but that had quickly been dashed to pieces when he convinced the editor at his previous job to run an article exposing a very high-profile Missouri senator as being a cheater who had slept around on his wife. The only problem was that the "concrete evidence" Lenny had presented to his boss was completely fabricated. When the senator caught wind of the article, he sued Lenny and the paper into the ground. It took him years to even get a paper to take him in at all. When the editor at the Inquisitor did give him a chance, it was made clear to him that he would never be allowed to write anything more than the occasional fluff piece and other mundane articles. So, while he had resigned himself to being the company whipping-boy, he also kept his ear to the ground, surrounding himself with as many sleazy contacts and sources as he could. He dreamed of one day blowing the lid off a major scandal and earning himself a spot as a news giant like Larry King or Walter Cronkite.

As he leaned back in his chair, making it squeak loudly again, his desk phone rang. His chubby sausage fingers fumbled to pick up the receiver, but he finally managed, and holding it to his ear, he said plainly, "Horowitz."

A gruff voice on the other end replied, "Hey, Lenny, it's Toad."

"Oh, hey, Donovan. What's up?"

"Got something you might be interested in over here at the shop, Lenny."

"Oh, really? What's that?"

"Don't really wanna talk about it over the phone, but let's just say it might be what you've been waiting for. Can you come down here so we can talk?"

"Maybe, but if I come down there, this better be legit, Toad. The last time I came down there, you wasted my time."

"I already apologized for that, asshole. Just get down here, Horowitz. I promise it will be worth it."

Lenny hung up the phone. Half an hour later, he was downtown, huffing and waddling his way into "22nd Street Gold and Pawn." The small metal bell made his presence known as he lumbered through the front door. He made it to one of the glass counters with a white backer filled with jewelry and other valuables, and stood there, catching his breath. Several minutes passed before the bead curtain covering the doorway to the back was disturbed. Lenny couldn't see anyone, but he heard footsteps coming toward him, then a voice asked, "That you, Lenny?" Lenny looked over the top of the counter to see a thin, dark-complected little person looking up at him. "Hey, Toad. How's it hanging?"

"Short and shriveled as always, you fat slob," Toad quipped, sneering at Lenny.

Toad Donovan was one of Lenny's main contacts. If anything sleazy or underhanded happened in KC, Toad knew about it. He was the owner-operator of this shady little pawn shop, so he got all the dirt from the local losers and troublemakers. He also knew many people in the organized crime business, making him the perfect person for Lenny to use to get his future blockbuster story. He even looked the part. He got his nickname from the fact that he had a large head and bugged-out eyes. That, mixed with his short stature and raspy voice, made it an obvious choice. It was Lenny who had given him the moniker, and Donovan had embraced it rather than get upset. He was also a mean, conniving little ass, so he and Lenny had gotten along almost immediately upon meeting for the first time.

"So, you ready to see what I got for you, fat boy?" Toad said with a sneer.

"I guess. This better not be another dud, Lollipop Guild," Lenny replied plainly.

"Follow me to the back. Can't show you here."

Toad walked to the front door and flipped the hanging sign to the "Closed" position, and started making his way to the back. Lenny followed close behind after sucking in his enormous gut to wiggle behind the counter. They passed through the bead curtain, and it rattled loudly as Lenny's huge torso parted the strings of plastic ovals. They followed a short hallway and ended up at Toad's office. The minuscule man went over to a small safe on the floor, spun the number dial left, right, then left again, and pulled the lever. The door swung open, and Lenny peeked over his shoulder to see what was inside. There was a small pile of papers, a few stacks of one-hundred-dollar bills, and a small plastic tab sitting on top of it all. Toad grabbed the red plastic object, which Lenny now saw was a flash drive, and walked over to a laptop on a messy table. Without a word, he fired up the PC and, once it booted, inserted the flash drive into the USB port on the side. He moved the cursor to the correct icon to open the file, then looked back at Lenny.

"Listen, Lenny. Before I open this file, prepare yourself for what you'll see. It's a video file that someone brought to me. The contents ain't pretty, and it's violent as fuck. Also, the person who brought this to me wants to remain anonymous, so don't even try to ask me who gave it to me. What's more, if you use this in any way, I don't want to be named either, because the one thing I can tell you about this person is that they're not someone you wanna fuck with. So, unless you want the two of us to end up eating a bullet buffet, I suggest you keep your mouth shut on your sources."

"What the fuck have you got your hands on, Donovan?" Lenny asked with anticipation and a hint of fear.

"You'll see," is all Toad said in response. Then he clicked the file, and the video played. "Remember the two FBI agents and all those cops that got massacred a few days ago?"

"No shit, I remember, Toad. How the fuck could I forget something like that?" Lenny asked sharply. "It was all over the news for Christ's sake!"

"Well," Toad replied, "You're about to get a front row seat to the main event and the name of the anonymous lead agent that botched the entire investigation from start to finish. Is that good enough to get you your ticket to the top, Doughboy?"

"Wait. What? How?"

"Don't worry about that. The only thing you need to worry about now is getting this out into the open for the whole world to see, Lenny."

"What's in this for you, Donovan? You aren't doing this out of kindness. Shit! You don't even have a heart!"

"Don't worry about me. I've already gotten my payment for this job. You make sure you hold up your end, or we're both cooked. Now sit back, grab your popcorn, and enjoy."

Toad pressed play on the video, and Lenny watched excitedly as the interior of a church appeared on the screen and a huge man in a black trench coat walked into the frame.

Chapter 11

Christmas Eve, One Year Later

Bud sat on the barstool, staring down at the untouched highball glass of amber liquid. His head was gently swaying left to right like a ship navigating the gentle waves of a mostly calm sea. Inside his head, however, a storm was raging. Beau had already walked over to check on him several times. He didn't want Beau or anybody else checking on him. He just wanted to be left the fuck alone. Alone to ponder, alone to feel sorry for himself, and alone to drink away all of the awful memories that haunted him like the ghosts of some long-forgotten Civil War battlefield haunted their dying grounds. He hadn't slept for two days now. He could never sleep anymore. The faces of all those whom he had lost made sure of that. Drinking didn't help, either, but he damn sure wasn't about to give that up again. It was about the only thing that he had left to numb the pain.

Then there were the memories of the article, the investigation, and their inevitable outcome. "How the fuck could it have happened?" he had thought to himself. First, there was the article. The headline had read, "Negligence and Cover-up in the FBI Leads to the Deaths of Two Agents and Thirteen Local Police Officers." Bud couldn't figure out for the life of him how someone had gotten their hands on actual video footage of the incident in the church that claimed the lives of both his partner and his boss, not to mention Detective Cho and his men. Even worse had been the fallout after. The new SAC, Michael Dixon, had slammed the paper down on his desk in front of Bud. He pointed stiffly and angrily at the front page.

"So what the fuck am I supposed to do with this mess, Barrett?! This is gonna be a goddamn media circus!"

The ass chewing would continue for almost an hour. All Bud could do was hang his head and take it. He already knew it was his fault, and he had no credible defense. Shortly after the meeting, the Internal Affairs investigation began. After weeks of pawing through all of the files about the church massacre and all of the other files tied to the KC Crusher case, they ultimately found that while Bud was not directly at fault for any of the problems that had occurred with the investigations, he was found guilty of conduct unbecoming of an agent for the drinking he had done the night his fellow agents died. They gave Bud a choice: he could either take an indefinite suspension without pay or quietly bow out of the agency with his benefits intact. He chose the latter.

So there he sat months later on Christmas Eve with a drink staring up at him mockingly, wondering where things had gone so wrong. He was so lost in thought that he hadn't even seen the man come in and sit down next to him, let alone speak to him. The man leaned further into Bud's view. He could see that the man's lips were moving, but his speech seemed muffled, like Bud's ears were stopped up by those little foam earplugs. Bud shook the cobwebs loose and looked at the man, still a little dazed.

"I'm so... sorry," Bud slurred. "Did you say something to me?"

"Well, since you're the only other soul in the bar at the moment, I would hope so. Otherwise, it means I'm talking to myself, and that wouldn't do at all," the man chuckled. "What I said was that this is some night to be drinking alone, wouldn't you agree?"

Bud eyed the man carefully, trying to read him, but his head was too fuzzy for that. What he did notice was that the man was tall and slender with stark white hair in bedhead style. His wire-framed glasses hung just off the bridge of his nose, but not in a sloppy way. He was square jawed, with a five o'clock shadow, and Bud supposed he was not unattractive. Bud even thought, in a strictly observational way, that the man was actually quite handsome. The man also spoke with a heavy British accent that reminded him of the way most upper-class Brits he had met spoke. He remembered someone once calling it "The Queen's English."

"Sorry, pal, but I prefer to drink alone these days," Bud politely, almost apologetically, replied.

"No offense meant, sir," the man replied, "and none taken. I'm Dansbury. Percival Dansbury, but most people call me Percy. And you are?" He extended an open palm to Bud.

"Someone who wants to be left to himself," Bud quipped more shortly. "Look, mister, Percy, I don't wanna be rude, but I'm not in the best of moods at the moment. Haven't been for a while. Besides, I could ask you the same question. Why are you in here alone on Christmas Eve?"

"Oh, I'm not alone," Percy replied with a slight smirk. "I'm meeting someone here."

Almost as if being summoned, the front door of the bar swung open wide, and Bud turned his head to see a stunningly beautiful woman glide into view.

Her light, almost ivory-colored skin shone softly in the low fluorescent lighting, and her wavy, jet-black hair flowed behind her. She was on the shorter side with a sturdy build, not muscular, but well-defined. She was also quite curvy, a quality Bud found quite attractive in a woman. He felt ashamed for a moment when he recalled Susan's curves. He blinked the memory away and kept watching the woman approach. One thing that really stood out was the way she was dressed. Bud thought it to be a tad on the chilly side for the woman to be wearing a baby tee and skin-tight leggings in the middle of winter, but then shrugged that thought off as well. She walked past Bud, eyeballing him a little, and then plopped down on the stool next to Percy.

"What's up, boys?" she asked in a bubbly, high-pitched New Jersey accent. "Who's buying me my first drink of the evening?"

Bud just stared at the odd pairing for a moment until Percy spoke to the woman without looking back at her.

"Delilah, I'd like you to meet...I'm sorry, I still haven't caught your name," he said to Bud.

"That's because I still haven't given it," Bud retorted.

"Geez, little grumpy, aren't you there, fella?" Delilah chimed in.

"Delilah," Percy responded, "Don't be rude to the man. It isn't the done thing. Isn't that right, Mr. Barrett?"

Bud immediately sobered.

"How the fuck did you..." Bud said sharply, a bit of confusion and alarm in his tone.

"Oh, come now, Bud. There's no need to get angry. I'm happy to explain how I know your name, along with a great many other things. We have a lot to talk about, the three of us," Percy responded evenly.

"Listen, mister, I don't know who the fuck you are and how you know who I am, but you better talk fast, or we're gonna have a serious fucking problem on our hands," Bud threatened.

"Ah, shit! Take the stick outta your ass, mister!" Delilah said in a slightly raised tone. "Ain't nobody gonna do a damn thing. Just calm down. As Percy said, we're gonna explain. Just give us a minute, will ya? Holy Moses on a rocket-powered pogo stick!"

"That's enough, Delilah," Percy said. "But she is right, Bud. Just give us a chance to explain."

"I'm done with your little game here, people. What are you? Reporters? Goddamn vultures! You lot haven't left me alone since that article came out! You finished off what was left of me! What are you doing now?! Coming back to pick the bones clean?!" Bud screamed, staggering to his feet.

Bud spun around to stagger out the door. As he took his first step, the front door swung open again. An extremely rotund man walked belly-first through the door, laughing loudly, followed closely by a round-faced, shady-looking little person. As Bud stopped to stare at them, the little person seemed to look past Bud, right at Percy and Delilah. "Oh shit!" The small man yelped. He immediately spun on his heel and began to run back out the door.

Percy, still not looking back, said, "Delilah, would you please be so kind as to stop our minuscule friend from getting too far?"

Delilah immediately jumped up and quickly sprinted out the door past both Bud and the fat man.

"You!" Bud spat with drunken venom in his voice. "I'm gonna beat your ass!" He had recognized the man immediately when he sauntered through the door. It was the bastard who had completely ruined his life with a single news article, Lenny Horowitz. Bud took a meaningful stride forward.

"Oh, fuck! Not you!" Horowitz said with a trembling voice. "Stay the fuck away from me!"

He turned to follow Delilah and his friend out the front door, but Bud closed the distance quickly. He knocked the huge man over, which wasn't very hard to do, considering his high center of gravity, and then he was on top of him. Bud began raining down blows on Lenny, connecting with his head and ribs repeatedly. Beau shouted something from behind the counter, but Bud couldn't hear it. A few seconds passed, and then Bud felt a strong pair of hands grip his shoulders and wrench him backwards. He landed flat on his back and peered up, expecting to see Beau standing over him. Instead, he saw Percy, who glared at him with disapproval.

"Mr. Barrett!" Percy shouted. "I think that will be quite enough of that!"

Horowitz stood up and cried out, "Oh, I'm gonna sue your ass and have you thrown in jail now, you prick!"

"You will do nothing of the sort, you fat waste of space!" Percy barked. "Or so help me, I will help Mr. Barrett up and let him finish what he started. Is that quite clear? Now, I suggest you leave and keep your mouth shut." Percy spoke with such authority and fire that all Horowitz could do was nod his head and shuffle away.

"What the fuck do you think you're doing, mister?" Bud yelled at Percy. "He had that beating coming after what he did! He ruined what was left of my life!"

"Oh, I'm fully aware of what he and his little cohort did, Bud. That's why Delilah and I are here. Also, I would ask that you speak to me with a little more respect, seeing as how I most likely just kept you from catching an assault charge and a sizeable lawsuit."

"Who are you, really?" Bud asked as Percy helped him to his feet and straightened his shirt. "Why are you really here, and how do you know about what's been going on in my life?"

"As I said, Mr. Barrett, the three of us have much to discuss, and Delilah and I have some things to show you as well. Before we do, can I assume that we aren't going to end up in a similar position with you as Mr. Horowitz just did?"

"I'm sorry," Bud said earnestly. "You have my word. It's just that I'm really confused and need answers."

Percy clapped Bud on the shoulder and said with a smile on his face, "And I promise you'll have them, my friend, but first, we need to go find Delilah and the little coward. Sound good?"

As the two of them left the bar, Bud looked back at Beau, who had a look of extreme confusion on his face. He could tell his old bartender buddy was at a loss for what had happened. "Sorry about the dust-up, Beau," Bud said sheepishly. "Yes, sorry about that," Percy added.

Beau scratched his head for a minute and then smiled. "Ah, shit, Bud. I wish you had finished that slimeball off after what he did. You two fellas have a good night and stay outta trouble." Beau watched as the two men disappeared into the night.

Chapter 12

Delilah called out to Bud and Percy from the alley beside the bar. "Back here, boys," she yelled out from the darkness. "I got him! The little asshole tried to knife me, but I got him!" Bud started sprinting to her, clearly worried for her safety, but Percy strolled casually behind like a man taking an after-dinner walk through the park. Bud cut through the darkness of the alley until he could see her and the little person, dimly illuminated by the soft glow of an incandescent light bulb hanging above the bar's side employee entrance. Delilah had the man in a chokehold, squeezing his throat tightly against her well-toned forearm. She was slightly lifting him off the ground so that his toes were barely touching the pavement. A small, silver-bladed dagger was lying beside the pair. Delilah wore a look of annoyance and amusement. The man was making squeaky gasping noises from the headlock being applied.

"Are you hurt?" Bud inquired of Delilah in a genuine tone.

"Nah," she replied. "Short little prick would need a stepladder to cut my throat with his pig-sticker."

"Language, please, Delilah," Percy chimed in as he finally caught up to the others.

"Some friend you are," Bud said to Percy.

"I assure you, Mr. Barrett, there was no need to worry about Delilah. She is more than capable of handling herself," Percy retorted.

"Delilah, would you be so kind as to stop strangling our diminutive friend? I would very much like to talk to him, and I'm afraid that's quite impossible in his current state; you know, with him not being able to breathe and all."

Delilah looked at Percy for a moment, continuing to squeeze down with her arm, and then, with some hesitance, released her grip. The man flopped to the ground, dropping straight to his knees and gasping for air in labored gulps. After a moment, he looked up at Delilah and muttered, "Bitch." Delilah made a move to snatch him back up again, but Percy intervened by snapping, "Mr. Donovan, that is no way to speak to a lady, especially not one that could crack your neck like a twig." Slowly getting to his feet, the man narrowed his eyes at Percy and, not looking back at Delilah, apologized in a tone clearly not sincere.

"That's better," Percy stated plainly. "Now, to business."

"Okay. Hold the fuck up a minute!" Bud interrupted. I am getting really tired of all this pretense and bullshit. Will one of you please tell me what the fuck is going on?! I've only known the two of you for half an hour, and you're already giving me a headache bigger than the worst hangover I've ever had!"

"As you wish, Mr. Barrett. No need to get your knickers in a twist. I was just about to do that anyway," Percy said in a reserved tone. "The living piece of excrement you see before you is Toad Donovan."

"The pleasure is all yours," Toad sneered, drawing a sharp smack to the back of the head from Delilah that almost took him off his feet again. "Quiet, short stack, or the next time you're losing some Chiclets."

Percy glared at the pair briefly, and they both shrank a little. "As I was saying, this is Toad Donovan, a small-time pawnbroker and big-time slimeball to the underworld of Kansas City. He has connections to every thief, murderer, and general psychopath that this town has to offer, but that's not why I had Delilah chase him down."

"Go on," Bud said with a hint of skepticism and interest in his voice.

"The reason I had Delilah detain him is that he has direct involvement in your current predicament."

"What's that supposed to mean?" Bud asked, this time with a little more fire.

"Well," Percy began again, "The long and the short is that he supplied the surveillance video of what happened at the church to Lenny Horowitz."

Bud's face instantly became beet-red as he tried to charge Toad. "You little son of a bitch! I'll kill you!" he screamed as he reached out for him.

With lightning reflexes, Percy stepped between the pair and stopped Bud dead in his tracks. "Mr. Barrett, control yourself!" he shouted. Bud halted and stared a hole through Percy and straight into Toad. Bud's breathing was heavy and strained, like a racehorse in the last turn of The Kentucky Derby. Rage radiated from his entire body, which visibly shook while he labored to restrain himself.

"You'll get a chance at justice soon enough, but it won't be tonight," Percy stated in his usual even tone. Delilah stepped to the side, silent but never taking her eyes away from their captive. She already seemed bored with the conversation and leaned against the exterior wall of the bar, crossing her legs at the ankles. Bud finally steadied himself and took a single step back.

Percy continued. "Bud, there are more things at play against you than you realize. It's time you knew the whole truth of the evils that have befallen you for the past few years." Percy stepped closer to Toad and said in a flat, yet irritated tone, "Tell him, Toad. You know who I am and what I'm capable of doing. You know that I already know everything about you and who you're working for right now. Just make this easy on everyone here and tell him."

"Go fuck yourself, twink! You don't scare me nearly as bad as who I'm working for, so get bent!" Toad barked.

Percy stared menacingly at Toad now, a look that up until this point, Bud hadn't thought him capable of in the slightest. "Well, then, I guess it's up to me to expose the man behind the curtain," he replied. He reached into the inner pocket of his tailored jacket and produced a small item. Bud looked closely, trying to identify it. It appeared to be a simple wooden cross, but the wood was blackened slightly, as if it had been burnt at some point in the past. He nodded to Delilah. In a flash, she was behind Toad again, grabbing him in a tight bear hug and lifting him from the ground. She had his arms pinned to his sides, and he was squirming in vain to break her grip.

"What the hell are you doing, Percy?" Bud asked, confused.

"This is how it starts, Bud," Percy replied, and he stepped closer to Toad. He held up the cross and spoke in a language that Bud immediately identified as Latin. Toad screamed in fear. Bud watched the scene, mouth agape, not knowing how to react. Percy placed the cross against Donovan's forehead and continued spouting the Latin phrases. The only word Bud was familiar with in the exchange so far was "Christus," Latin for "Christ." He watched in amazement as the cross began to spark and smoke until it burst into flames against Toad's skin. The little man cried out in immense pain.

"Stop it!" Bud shouted. "Stop it! You're going to kill him! This has gotten out of hand!" Even as the words left his mouth, Bud realized to his astonishment something that he hadn't before noticed. While the cross seemed to be scorching Toad's skin, the hand that Percy was using to hold the cross was seemingly untouched by the fire, and Percy himself seemed unaffected. The cross was only hurting Toad. "What the fuck?" Bud thought to himself. The very next instant, he was left in complete and utter shock. He watched in disbelief, and Toad's skin began to melt away, but not from the flames that were engulfing his head. Not only that, but Toad's entire body began to writhe and shift.

Bones and joints began to pop in and out of place as they shifted into new positions. When the process had completed, Delilah was no longer holding Toad Donovan in her arms, but a small, hideous, red-skinned creature with an unnaturally wide mouth full of razor-sharp teeth and small wings that were pressed against Delilah's chest.

"Jesus Christ," Bud thought to himself, and as if hearing his thoughts, the creature replied, "Not even fucking close!" It grinned with a sickening countenance that made a chill run all the way up Bud's spine. "What the fuck is that thing?" he asked no one in particular.

"This piece of trash," Delilah began, finally breaking her silence, "Is an imp, and a particularly nasty little fucker by the name of Crag."

"An imp?" Bud stammered. "They, they exist? What the fuck? How the fuck do they actually exist? I always thought that shit like this only happened in fairytales."

"I assure you, Bud," Percy interjected, "They are quite real, along with many other nasty entities that go bump in the night. That, Mr. Barrett, is the real reason that Delilah and I are here. Well, that, and to help you on your path." "Path to what?" Bud asked, even more confused.

"Why, your path to redemption, of course," Percy responded, a slight smirk on his face. "Now, I'm afraid we have a tad more to reveal, so brace yourself. Delilah, if you would be so kind."

Bud looked to Delilah. While still holding the imp tightly in her grasp, she closed her eyes, bowed her head for a moment, and then looked directly at Bud. Her eyes glowed a fantastic magenta, and with a wink, she was suddenly surrounded by a swirling black shadow that reminded Bud of a miniature tornado. When the shadows dissolved a moment later, Bud found himself staring at one of the most frighteningly beautiful entities he had ever seen. Her skin was a deep shade of purple, and she had large, onyx colored wings extending from her back, almost in the same fashion as those on the imp, but more well-formed. Her face was the same as before, but somehow Bud felt within himself that it was even more stunning now. She was adorned in a silky dress that reminded him of the little cocktail dress Susan used to wear to charity events and parties at the FBI offices. By far, though, the most striking thing Bud noticed about the creature in front of him was her presence. There seemed to be an aura surrounding her that pulsed with what he could only feel was raw sexual energy. It was completely intoxicating to him, almost to the point where he could keep his wits about him. "Let's keep it simple, honey," Delilah said to Bud. "You're a smart fella. I'm sure you know what a succubus is, don't ya?" Bud could only nod slightly as his brain tried to catch up with his eyes. "Well, that's me in a nutshell," she said with a wink, and a smirk crossed her face.

"Well, I guess last but not least," Percy started. Bud turned his attention to the prim and proper Brit, only to think at first that Percy hadn't changed. He only stood there with his head bowed slightly. Suddenly, he opened his eyes wide to reveal a blinding white light from deep within them, so bright, in fact, that Bud had to shield his own eyes. The light subsided, and in one swift, fluid motion, Percy unfolded a perfectly formed set of ivory-toned wings stretching out from his back in a huge arc. He folded them back in against his body and stepped towards Bud, who trembled slightly at his approaching form. "Don't be afraid, Mr. Barrett. As I mentioned earlier, Delilah and I are here to support you on your journey. God has a task for you, and as your guardian angel, I intend to make sure you complete it. Come with us, Bud. We have much more to show you, and we must find Captain Ivan Novikoff. Your life, and the lives of all humankind, depend on it."

Chapter 13

The deadbolt lock on the apartment door slid open. The door swung ajar, and Lenny stepped over the threshold. He flicked his hand to the right, and his keyring clanged into a jade-colored porcelain bowl sitting on top of a small end table. Without even bothering to turn on the lights, he turned to the left and slowly shuffled through the kitchen to his refrigerator. He grabbed a bag of peas from the freezer and gently applied them to his face. "That damned FBI asshole really did a number on me," he thought to himself. He then supposed that it could have been worse if that stranger in the bar hadn't called off the dogs. Barrett might have actually killed him. He leaned back against the fridge and let out a pained sigh.

"Mr. Horowitz," a voice cooed from the darkness. "So nice to finally meet you in person."

Lenny jumped and barked out a noise that sounded like a mixture of a gasp and a grunt. "What the fuck?" he yelled. "Who the fuck is in my house, and what do you want? I'm warning you, I'm armed!" He ran for the light switch by the door and slapped it on, looking frantically around for the intruder.

"You most certainly are not armed," said the large man sitting in Lenny's favorite recliner. "Besides, even if you

were armed, it would do you no good in this particular moment."

Now trembling, Lenny asked again, "Who the fuck are you and what do you want?"

My name is Captain Ivan Novikoff, and I am looking for a mutual associate of ours by the name of Toad Donovan," he said as he stood. The Russian strolled casually toward Lenny. He towered over the robust reporter and peered down at him as Lenny pushed all the way back against the kitchen sink.

"Wait," Lenny replied. "You're the Russian guy Toad was telling me about?"

"Da," Novikoff replied. "I need to speak to him about some urgent business, but when I went to his pawn shop tonight, he wasn't there. Since you are the person he most often spends time with, I was hoping I could find him here."

"How the fuck did you even know where my apartment was?" Horowitz asked.

"That's not important, Mr. Horowitz. What is important is that you tell me where Mr. Donovan is so that we can complete our business."

"I, I don't know where he is," Lenny replied shakily.

Novikoff's brow furrowed, showing signs of obvious frustration. "What do you mean you don't know?" he asked in a much darker tone. "Were you with him tonight?"

"Yeah, I was for a little bit. We grabbed some burgers and then headed over to Beau's Place for a few beers. It's a little dive joint that we drink at all the time."

"Did you part ways there?" the huge Russian inquired.

"Well, sorta." Lenny shifted uneasily. "See, we had just walked through the door when we ran into some trouble."

Ivan's face grew even darker, and his tone became more impatient as he asked, "What do you mean you ran into trouble? Mr. Horowitz, where is Toad?"

Lenny broke into a sweat, and his legs grew wobbly. His voice began to quiver as he stared up at the now obviously angry giant. He broke. "It wasn't my fault! One minute, we were laughing and cutting up, and the next minute, that damned FBI agent had me on the ground and was pounding my fucking face! He probably would have beaten me to death, but some nerdy-looking prick got him off of me. Toad must have seen the guy before I did, because he split as soon as the whole thing started! While I was on the ground, I heard the nerdy guy tell his bitch to go after him. After he let me up, I got the hell out of Dodge."

The Russian growled with rage and put his fist through the cabinet next to Lenny's head. It gave way with a thunderous crash, and chunks of wood flew in every direction. "What FBI Agent?!" Novikoff howled.

Lenny was cowering almost to the floor. "The one we exposed, you know, Bud Barrett."

Novikoff grabbed up Lenny by the shirt and lifted him until his feet were no longer touching the ground. "And you just left Toad there with them?!" He began shaking Lenny like a rag doll. "I should..." He composed himself and abruptly sat Horowitz down. "I apologize for my outburst, Lenny. May I call you Lenny?" His face had begun to soften.

Lenny looked down to see that there was a small puddle of urine under his feet. He stammered, "Uh, yeah. Yeah. You can call me Lenny." He waited breathless for a response.

"Lenny, I need you to think very hard for me." He paused. "You said that there were two people with the agent, a man and a woman, yes? Can you describe them for me in as much detail as possible?"

Lenny recalled for a moment and then said, "Yeah. The man was tall and slender. He was wearing a really nice-looking three-piece suit and glasses. He had white hair in a modern-style cut. He spoke with a British accent."

"And the woman?" asked the Russian evenly.

"Didn't really get a good look at her. She ran out the door pretty quickly when Toad ran off. She didn't say anything, but I can tell ya this: she was hot. The rack and ass on this broad. Wow! She had black hair and was wearing tight leggings and one of those t-shirts that looks like it's two sizes too small."

"Percy and Delilah," the large man muttered

to himself. "Who the fuck is that?" Lenny asked.

"None of your concern," Novikoff said. "Thank you for your cooperation, Mr. Horowitz. I'll be leaving now. You've been quite helpful. If I could, might I ask you for one last favor?"

"Sure," Lenny said warily.

Novikoff grinned. "Well, I need someone to deliver a message to Mr. Barrett and his two companions."

"You can fucking forget that!" Lenny shouted in an almost laughing tone. "I'm not going anywhere near that psycho again!"

"I believe you misunderstand, Mr. Horowitz. I didn't say I needed all of you to relay the message. I only need part of you!"

Novikoff snatched Lenny by the collar and pulled him in close. Reaching inside his own shirt, the Russian pulled out a strange-looking amulet. He held it to Lenny's forehead. He began muttering phrases to himself in a language Lenny had never heard. As his head began to swim, the last thing Lenny Horowitz ever heard was the sound of a guttural growl from behind him.

Chapter 14

As the whisps of flurried snow danced past the large bay windows, Bud sat in his armchair, silent and motionless. He wondered to himself if he was actually experiencing all of the events of tonight, or if it was all some big fever dream brought on by a touch of the flu or the hair of the dog. Had he really just seen what he thought he saw? "What the actual fuck?" he asked internally. "Is Percy really my guardian angel, a real-life, honest-to-God angel? Is he really running around with a slutty demon in disguise? What the hell does any of this have to do with me, and what the hell makes me so special that God himself has chosen me to complete some task?" His mind was racing, almost to the point of making him nauseated.

As if reading Bud's mind, Percy spoke up. "I know this is all happening extremely fast, Bud, but God assigned me to you and sent me to you with a most urgent and important task. This task could mean the survival of humankind, or its extinction. Only time will tell, Mr. Barrett, time and you." As he spoke, Delilah looked on from the edge of Bud's bed with an expression that either suggested amusement or mischief. Bud couldn't decide which it was, maybe a little of both.

"I still don't have any idea what any of this has to do with me, Percy," Bud replied, a mixture of worry and confusion in his tone.

Percy sighed. "It will take too long to explain, Bud. It's best that you see for yourself." He rose from the edge of the kitchen island that he had been leaning against and took a step towards the former FBI agent.

"Stay back!" Bud shouted. "Don't come near me! I saw what you did to that imp in the alley. You turned him into a Godamn pile of dust!"

Percy halted. "Bud, I told you, he was never going to tell us where Novikoff was hiding or what he planned next, and I wasn't about to let him go so that he could warn him that we had found you!"

"Besides," Delilah chimed in, "that little prick had it coming. Little asshole tried to knife me! Don't be such a pussy, Buddy boy." She smirked and winked at Bud.

"Delilah, dear, I thought we had an agreement about your use of curse words," Percy said in his usual even tone.

"Well, excuse the mother fucking, corn-holing shit outta me, Percy!" This time, she broke into a full-blown smile.

Percy turned his attention back to Bud. "Bud, you have to trust me. I promise that I'm not going to hurt you, but you have to see for yourself." He stood stoically, waiting for Bud's decision.

Bud sat in thought for a few moments and then said, "Fine. Just do whatever it is that you're going to do quickly before I change my mind."

Percy slowly approached Bud, bent slightly to meet his eyes, and lightly touched his index and middle fingers to Bud's forehead. Bud's eyes rolled back in his head, and images began to flash white-hot in his mind. They were coming and going so fast that Bud's mind was starting to swirl and blur. For a moment, he felt like he might even vomit. When he came to, he felt like he had been trapped in his own mind for an eternity. In actuality, it had only been for a few minutes. His head pounded worse than the nastiest migraine he had ever experienced. When the fog had finally cleared, Bud sat in both amazement and fear at the things he had seen and heard. It all played out like a movie in his mind. Bud quickly learned that humanity had gotten its origin story *very* wrong.

In the beginning, the gods had created the heavens and the earth. Chiefest among them were The Ten: Jehovah, Zeus, Odin, Ra, The Goddess, Brahma, Yu Huang, Bondye, Jupiter, and Itzamna. They existed in perfect harmony with their individual followers, including angels, spirits, and other lesser gods or deities. One day, Jehovah, the most powerful among the Ten, proposed to the others that they should create a race of beings to worship them, thereby strengthening their powers and longevity. At first, the other gods balked at the idea, asking Jehovah why they would need such creations. Jehovah stated that even they would grow lonely and weary of each other's company after a time, and that if they had other beings with free will to change continually and progress, the gods would have a stronger purpose to their own existence. Eventually, the other gods agreed to help Jehovah create the race of man, on the condition that each would receive an equal share of worshipers throughout humanity's time on earth. So the process of creating humanity began.

While the gods toiled to create the complex race known as humans, some among their followers resisted the notion that the gods could love such lowly beings. Rumors began to swirl among them that one of the most powerful and beautiful angels of Jehovah, Lucifer by name, was extremely angry and had begun talks with some of the generals of the gods' armies to overthrow them and strike down the humans as soon as they were created. As an extremely charismatic and convincing figure, he quickly turned rumors into truth as he began to sway some of the generals to his way of thinking. Lucifer plotted with the generals of each god's army to assassinate their leaders in a coordinated attack; once dead, their essences would be consumed by the angel, making him powerful enough to confront Jehovah himself. With Lucifer's amassed forces behind him, Jehovah would fall, and he would become the new ruler of the heavens and earth.

Time is fluid in the heavens. While Lucifer made his plans and poisoned the gods' armies against them, humanity had come into its own. Civilizations rose and fell, and people scattered to, and inhabited, every corner of the earth. Lucifer, to that point, had convinced all but three of the generals to side with him in his uprising. He was still trying to persuade the followers of Bondye, the Earth Goddess, and Jehovah to join his cause when two events forced him to hasten his attack. First, word had reached him that Jehovah's human followers had begun to stray from him, causing him to send a messiah to his worshippers. Known as Jesus of Nazareth, this messiah would replenish Jehovah's power by strengthening his followers' faith. Second, a spy had told Lucifer that his brother, Michael, had caught wind of his plans and was coming to confront him soon. Lucifer decided the time to act was now. He sent word to his conspirators that it was time to launch the attacks.

One by one, the gods fell at the hands of their own followers, and a great battle ensued in the heavens. Eventually, the successful assassinations of the gods led Lucifer to gather the essences of seven of the ten gods to himself. Then came the turning point. The armies of the three remaining gods managed to stem the tide of war and started to beat back the assault. Then, Michael came for Lucifer. The battle raged between the two celestial brothers for what seemed like an eternity. During the fight, Michael's onslaught caused Lucifer to lose the essences of the seven fallen gods, which were scattered across the earth. Eventually, Michael got the better of his brother by slashing him with a sword made of pure light, causing Lucifer to lose some of his own essence in the process. Weakened, Lucifer was cast into a hellish prison by the archangel, and to ensure he remained weakened, Michael found the essence his brother had lost in the fight and sealed it within a unique talisman. He rejoined the armies of the three remaining gods, and eventually pushed back the enemy until they scattered to the ends of the earth and went into hiding. However, even though Lucifer was trapped in his prison, he was still able to communicate with his agents who were in hiding. He commanded them to scour the earth for the seven essences that were lost to him, plus his own that Michael stole. Once back in his possession, Lucifer would be able to break from his cage and challenge the three remaining gods again.

Meanwhile, knowing his brother's heart, Michael implored Jehovah to hide the essence of Lucifer among the most trusted of his followers, so that he might never find it. Jehovah commanded Michael to entrust the Talisman of Lucifer to one of Jesus of Nazareth's disciples. A short time after the crucifixion of Jesus, Michael had his brother Gabriel approach the disciple known as Jude, knowing that his heart was pure and his intentions were noble. Gabriel relayed the story of the talisman to Jude, who swore to hide and protect it, along with all who were of his lineage. Jude took the talisman and hid it among his people. For years, the talisman remained hidden, keeping Lucifer from ever having the chance to rise.

Then, during the Second Great War between the different countries of the world, the talisman fell into the hands of an evil dictator by the name of Adolf Hitler. He was obsessed with the supernatural and collected the gods' artifacts like trophies. However, his possession of the talisman was short-lived. The end came for Hitler and those who followed him at the hands of a group of allied countries. Through the fall of Hitler's forces, the talisman was discovered by an American soldier who took it as a souvenir, not knowing its significance. Seeing these things come to pass, Jehovah sent Gabriel to the American who had taken the talisman to a town called Boston,

Massachusetts. Gabriel revealed himself and the talisman's importance to the soldier, and, as a man of faith, the soldier promised to hide it again somewhere safe. The soldier took the talisman to the safest place he could think of, entrusting it to his own priest, Father Hansen of St Augustine Catholic Church. "Have faith, Thomas Barrett," the priest said in comfort to the soldier. "God will prevail."

Chapter 15

Percy and Delilah

Percy walked down the cold, silent Boston street. The wind was whipping wildly in his face, and his eyes began to water slightly. There wasn't another soul on the street. "Silent as a graveyard," he thought to himself. Wasn't that the expression humans used? He shook his head vacantly and huffed out a cloud of foggy breath into the night air. He continued down the sidewalk, nothing but the sound of his own shoes smacking the pavement to keep him company. He finally stopped in front of a small, two-story house on the corner of McGuire and Wilson. There was nothing especially magnificent about the home. In fact, it looked the same as every other home on the street. However, Percy had learned a long time ago that looks can be deceiving. Inside, he knew, something extremely special was happening. It was 1990, and inside the home at 1725 East Wilson Avenue, Lilly Louise Barrett was giving birth to the child whom Percy already knew would be named Buddy Thomas Barrett; Buddy because, well, Lilly liked the name Buddy, and Thomas because his father Bill wanted to name him after his late grandfather.

Percy wondered, staring blankly at the dull white vinyl siding and the blue shudders lining the double-paned windows, if this was really how things had to be. Was Jehovah certain that this was the only way to stop Lucifer from rising to power and eliminating the three remaining gods residing in the heavens? How would this innocent, newborn child become the only man in existence to be able to deal with the burden of saving the world from the wrath and rage of a fallen angel? He already knew the answers to these questions because Jehovah had already explained.

The progression of man, Jehovah had told him, had not gone the way the gods had originally planned. As centuries passed, man grew increasingly selfish, brutal, and savage, growing weaker in his faith in the gods with each passing day. It had also become panicked and distrustful of the supernatural and of anything it couldn't immediately explain. Thus, humanity as a whole could no longer be trusted, and neither the gods nor their followers could openly reveal themselves to people as they once could. So when Father Hansen lost the talisman to the hands of a particularly nasty follower of Lucifer by the name of Ivan Novikoff, Jehovah set a plan in motion to secretly regain the talisman, with humanity being none the wiser, thus avoiding mass hysteria and panic and ending Lucifer's hopes of rising at the same time. However, there was a major problem.

When Novikoff took possession of the talisman, Lucifer somehow managed to use what limited power he had to cloak it from the eyes of the gods, making it impossible to track from the heavens. The only solution was to have someone physically track and retrieve the talisman on Earth. For years, Percy looked for Novikoff alone, always seemingly one step behind. Wearing the talisman cloaked his movements, gave the Russian freakish strength, speed, and agility, and halted the aging process. He had essentially stayed the same age since 1947, when he had found the talisman. Percy had learned he was originally meant to take it back to a Russian dictator named Stalin. Still, once the sadistic man had seen what the talisman did for him, he had apparently decided to keep it for a time to play out his evil desires before ultimately returning it to his master. Novikoff wasn't a demon, but he may as well have been.

Feeling defeated, Percy reported back to Jehovah that his attempts to find Novikoff had been fruitless. So, Jehovah and the other two remaining gods devised a plan to stop Novikoff once and for all. When Buddy's grandfather, Thomas, took possession of the Talisman of Lucifer during the war, he showed a natural resilience to it that no one else had ever shown while it was hidden. While the men to whom it had originally been entrusted had not completely fallen to its temptations, they were constantly tested. However, Thomas Barrett was a devout man who never wavered in his faith. Unfortunately, his son Bill did not take up his father's mantle. Bill Barrett was a heavy drinker, and the gods knew that his vices would lead to his downfall, which they eventually did. Knowing this, the gods pinned their hopes on the next in line, Bill's son Buddy. Knowing the importance of keeping the child safe, Jehovah sent Percy to watch over him as his guardian angel, guiding him from a distance until the day came when he could reveal himself to Buddy, as part of the gods' plan.

So here Percy stood, listening to the commotion within the quaint little home of Bill and Lilly Barrett, and feeling a combination of both fear and hope for the future.

"You still trust the big guy's plan?" a perky female voice asked from behind Percy.

"You know I do, Delilah," Percy replied wearily.

"Then why the fuck are you standing here like a brokenhearted teenage boy at the house of the girl that left him?" Delilah quipped. She walked up to him and placed a hand on his shoulder.

"Language, please," he replied flatly. "I don't know. I just have this feeling that I can't shake that things aren't going to go as smoothly as we think."

Percy looked at her with tired eyes. She smiled back at him and gave him a wink. "Can you please unclench that uptight British asshole of yours for five minutes? I mean, I get that you're just staying in the visage you created, but you're actually starting to sound like one of those limey pricks," she chuckled. He laughed lightly in return.

Delilah always knew how to make Percy feel better. She had such a sickeningly upbeat and perky attitude that it was infectious. Percy both hated and loved that, and she knew it, so she played it to her advantage every chance she got. She met Percy in Boston about three months into his original search for the talisman. She was roaming the streets of Beantown, also looking for the talisman, but not for the reason that Percy would at first think. Delilah had grown sick of constantly hiding from the followers of the gods, who popped in and out of the world, seeking the essences of the fallen gods and Lucifer's talisman. Being a strong-willed demon and never really trusting Lucifer at his word to begin with, she had come to hate the angelic dickhead, and she had only met him once. So when she ran into Percy, and the initial tussle between them had come to an abrupt end after discovering they were too evenly matched for either to prevail, they had a conversation. Delilah told Percy that since she "Hated Lucifer's sleazy guts and just wanted to be left alone," they agreed to work together until the talisman was found and Lucifer was defeated. However, over the years since they first met, Delilah had become very fond and protective of Percy. He was the only friend she had ever really had, and he didn't look at her like she was an enemy. She knew he saw her the same way as she saw him, and that made her happy. Well, it at least made her as happy as a former follower of Lucifer could be.

She was pretty sure that once old angel boy found out that she had betrayed him, he would have her skinned alive, stitched back together, and then skinned again. Wash, rinse, and repeat. She had told Percy this when they had first discussed teaming up, and he had agreed to keep it a secret from any others of their kind that they came across, good or bad, as long as she promised not to tell the gods that he was working with someone from the other side.

Delilah squeezed Percy's shoulder. "Come on, feather brains. This kid ain't gonna be ready to do shit for at least a few decades. Let me buy you a drink. We'll check back in on him a little later and then pick up the chase for our psycho. And if anybody so much as looks at the kid funny, I'll use their guts for a fucking garter belt."

"Delilah," Percy said as they began to walk down the street.

"Yeah, Percy?"

"Language."

Chapter 16

When Bud's eyes finally opened again, he was staring up at the white, textured ceiling of his studio apartment and the always mischievous grin of Delilah peering down at him. He immediately felt the oncoming surge of a horrific headache, one that throbbed incessantly, like someone had been operating a jackhammer right next to his ear for the last twenty-four hours. He also felt extremely nauseated, but since he hadn't eaten in quite some time, he was quite sure that he wouldn't have anything to throw up even if he tried. Every part of his head, neck, and shoulders was sore, like the times he passed out on the couch after an all-night bender. Simply put, Bud felt like a hammered dog shit.

"About time you woke the hell up," Delilah said in an unnecessarily sarcastic tone.

"Fuck," Bud replied groggily, "How long was I out?" He sat up just as Percy was looking at his watch.

"About two hours," Percy answered, in a matter-of-fact tone.

"Thought you were gonna stay passed out all night, sleeping beauty," Delilah returned.

Bud finally regained his wits and noticed he was in his bed, somehow wearing his pajamas. "Please don't tell me..."

"Relax, handsome," Delilah reassured him. "Old wet mop here changed you and spoiled my fun. From what I managed to peek at, though, you're not half bad, sailor." She winked at him and grinned.

"Really, Delilah?" Percy asked, looking exasperated. "Is that all you ever think about?"

"What else is there?" she remarked. "Not like we were gonna get anything done while Superman here was taking his big boy nap."

Bud interrupted the spat. "Can we focus here? Never mind the small details. Percy, what the hell did you do to me? My freaking head is on fire, and I feel like puking for a week straight."

"I just showed you what Jehovah needed you to see, Bud. That's all," Percy responded.

"What did he need me to see?! You still haven't explained what that means. Why did he show me all of that shit?!" Bud barked, clearly frustrated.

"You saw, so you know why, Buddy Boy,"
Delilah interrupted. "You saw everything and don't
act like you didn't. You saw the whole fucking shit
show!"

"Delilah..."

"Yeah, yeah, Percy, I know language. But for
fuck's sake! Can we get on with the important part
now?!" Delilah asked, also in clear frustration.

"Fine, Percy said plainly. "Let's proceed. Bud,
you know now what it is Jehovah and the other two
gods want from you. Are you ready to submit to that
cause?"

Bud sat and pondered for a moment, and
then finally relented with a deep sigh. "Ok, so let's
say I believe this mess of me being the chosen one or
whatever. What is the next step?"

Delilah chuckled lightly under her breath.
"You already took it, doll face."

"What the fuck does that mean, Delilah?"
Bud asked impatiently.

"It means that when P. put the whammy on
you, he also gave you what you need to take out that
Russian psycho."

Bud jerked his head to look at Percy, which was a clear mistake, and he let out a grimace from the too-sudden movement he made. "What the hell is she talking about?"

Percy looked at his feet, like a little boy being scolded by his father. "I'm sorry, Bud, but I had no choice. Right before I touched your forehead, Jehovah spoke to me. He told me time was running short, and we needed to act quickly. One of my brothers reported back to him that two of the essences of the fallen gods had been recovered by the enemy in Western Africa. He and a handful of the agents of Bondye fought to try to regain them quietly, but too much attention was being drawn by the fight, so they had to abandon the attempt. The enemies fled, but to where, we aren't sure. That means that there are only five left for them to retrieve now."

"Percy, what...the fuck...did you do?" Bud asked again, emphasizing each word.

"I followed Jehovah's plan. Bud, while you are more than capable of defending yourself against another normal human, Ivan Novikoff is not normal. Because of the talisman he bears, he is stronger, faster, and more agile than even the best athlete or soldier in the entire world. Jehovah knew that you could never defeat him one-on-one as a man, so he sent some aid to you."

"What kind of aid, Percy?"

"Bud, my brother Michael volunteered to help. He has more reason than most to ensure Lucifer never rises. So, when I touched you, Michael worked through me and transferred some of his power into you. Your body now contains some of the force of Michael the Archangel."

"I don't believe you," Bud quickly interjected. "There's no way that I'm worthy or strong enough to have..."

Bud's cellphone whirred on his nightstand, interrupting his thought. They all looked over at the small, rectangular device. Bud leaned over to check the contact. "Blocked Number" is all that it said. Bud looked back at Percy and Delilah for a moment, his brow furrowed. Then he reached over, pushed the "answer" button, and put the phone to his ear.

An out-of-breath voice wheezed into the phone; a voice that Bud thought sounded vaguely familiar. "Agent Barrett?" the voice inquired.

"Former agent Barrett," Bud corrected. "Who is this?"

"It's Lenny Horowitz. You know who I am. I need to talk to you. I assume the other two are there with you?"

Bud placed the phone on speaker. "What the fuck do you want, you piece of slime?" Bud growled into the phone.

"I know that you know who he is now: Ivan Novikoff. Look, I know you hate my guts, but that fucking psycho was in my apartment a while ago, and he tried to kill me! I barely escaped with my life!" His breaths became labored and ragged again. "I know what he's planning, but I need somewhere to hold up. I'm too exposed out here on the streets. If he finds me, he'll finish me off. You gotta help me, Barrett! If you hide me, I'll tell you everything I know!"

Bud looked back at Percy and Delilah. Percy nodded to him slightly, and Bud, gritting his teeth, nodded back to him. "Fine," he said into the phone. "Where are you so I can come get you?"

"Meet me at Beau's as soon as you can. I'm heading there now. Get here as quickly as you can. I think I lost him for now, but I don't know how long my luck will hold," Lenny said pleadingly.

"Fine," Bud replied. "But if this is some kind of double cross..."

"It's not! I swear!" Lenny snapped. "Just get to Beau's. Hurry before he finds me!" He disconnected the call.

Bud looked at Percy and Delilah and frowned. "I think we all know this is a setup, right?"

"Of course, the fuck it is!" Delilah quipped. "But that little piece of dick cheese needs to be dealt with, especially if he's working with Novikoff now. Either Novikoff will be there, or we can torture Horowitz to find out where he is." "We're not going to be torturing anyone, D.," Percy stated. "Just the same, we should be on high alert, and it looks like you're going to get a crash course in how to use your newfound powers, Mr. Barrett. Shift-on-the-fly, as they say? Right, let's get going."

Delilah skipped to the door like a little girl whose parents just told her they were taking her to the park, and Percy and Bud filed in behind her. "This is gonna be fun," she said in a gleeful tone. "Old Hornywitz is about to take it up the tailpipe."

Percy groaned, "Delilah, please."

Chapter 17

Bud sat in the back of Percy's cherry-red 1966 Corvette in complete silence. He was playing out the many scenarios that might unfold once they got to Beau's. Was this really a trap, or was Lenny really asking for help? Would Novikoff actually be there, or was he using Lenny as a pawn to catch them all off guard? Most importantly, would he finally get to confront the man who took his wife and daughter away from him, or was everything that had happened in the past few days going to end up being one big nightmare? Would he wake up and be in his bed, still stuck at square one on the haunting case that had eluded him? A thousand other thoughts swam through his mind at the same time.

Delilah snapped him out of his trance. She was sitting in the front seat, softly humming Wagner's Ride of the Valkyries to herself and swaying from side to side. Percy was driving, and Bud could tell he was trying his best not to say anything to Delilah about her humming. Bud could tell the pair had a very unique relationship. It was a good relationship, but also a strained one. Some might even say that it was a relationship of mutually assured destruction. They had come together in a pairing born out of need, but chaos breeds chaos, so the end would no doubt eventually come for them both sooner rather than later. Still, Percy, Bud surmised, wasn't opening his mouth to berate Delilah because he knew her little quirks and annoyances were just who she was. She needed the outlet.

Bud glanced down and noticed that he had absent-

mindedly been rubbing one of the beads of the rosary that Mya's mother had given him between his thumb and index finger. It immediately flashed the memory of the first time he had met her into his mind. Headstrong and foulmouthed, she could trash-talk just as well, if not better than, any of the male agents with whom they worked. A light smile spread across his face. It was short-lived, though, as his thoughts then jumped to the memory of the night that she and Charlie were taken from him, just like Susan and Lilly. The gory displays of his friends and family, splayed out before him, made him jump and shiver. Percy looked back at him through the rearview mirror.

"You feeling alright, chap?" Percy asked with concern.

"No," Bud answered. "But I will be once this thing plays out one way or the other."

"One way or the other," Delilah added. "Now there's a comforting thought. You fellas really know how to kill a girl's buzz, huh?"

Percy and Bud looked at her simultaneously and let out a light, unified chuckle. "Yup, that's us," Bud joked, "Always a way with the ladies."

Percy brought the car to a stop at a red light and looked back at Bud again. "Bud, when we get to the bar, things may escalate quickly, and I didn't really have a chance to go over the particulars of how to control the powers that Jehovah bestowed on you. The most important thing you must realize is that this isn't some comic book, and you aren't a superhero. You're not invincible. If you get caught flat-footed, you could very well die, and then all of our hopes of stopping Lucifer may go out the window." He paused for a moment to move the car as the light turned green. He took in a deep breath and exhaled slowly. "Utilizing the essence of an archangel isn't like turning a light switch on and off, and you're not inherently going to understand how to do it. The best advice I can give is: if things go south, stay behind Delilah and me until there's no other choice but to defend yourself. You have your sidearm with you, right?" Bud nodded. "Good. If a fight breaks out, try to use it to help either of us if we get overwhelmed. If the fight comes to you, all I can say is to trust in the gods, especially Jehovah, as he is the one you most closely associate with, to show you the way of things. You have my word that the two of us are willing to be destroyed in your defense should it come to that."

"Speak for yourself, P.," Delilah chirped. "If shit gets deep, I'm running like a little bitch!" Percy glared at her, and her face remained serious until it wasn't. She let out a burst of laughter. "I'm just fucking with ya, Percy! Have I ever let ya down before, Chicken Wing?" Percy rolled his eyes and turned another corner. He brought the car to a stop on the near end of Larkin Street, the street that held Beau's Place.

"Are you sure you're ready for this, chum?" Percy asked Bud plainly.

"As ready as I'm gonna be. This has been a long time coming, and if I can stop even one more person from being hurt by this guy, then I have to do it." He paused and slowly shook his head in disbelief. "Look at me. I'm a defamed, alcoholic former FBI agent who just got the biggest promotion ever. Savior of the entire goddamn universe. If mom could only see me now." He smirked.

"Well, Mr. Ego," Delilah responded sarcastically, "Let's go fuck shit up!"

Percy side-eyed Delilah for a moment and opened his mouth to correct her, but then said, "You know what, my dear? For once, I think your assessment of the situation is correct. Let's fuck shit up."

Bud and Delilah looked at Percy as if he had two heads for a moment, smiled, and then all three of the companions opened their car doors and stepped out onto the pavement. As they began down the sidewalk, they could barely make out the green haze of the green neon sign of Beau's. The street was silent and empty, except for a single homeless man pushing a shopping cart down the opposite sidewalk towards, and then away from, the trio. Once they looked back to see he was no longer in sight, Bud checked his pistol to make sure it was racked and ready. Delilah whipped her head from side to side, making it audibly crack like she was at a chiropractic appointment, and Percy just strolled casually as per his usual style. The three stopped in front of the bar entrance, looking up at the sign for a moment, and then up and down the street to make sure no one was watching them.

Percy whispered to Delilah, "Okay, my dear. You know what to do."

In the blink of an eye, Delilah had removed her human visage and shot straight up into the air in one fluid motion until she was out of sight. She soundlessly landed back in front of them a couple of minutes later and resumed her human form. "As far as I can see, there's no one at the back of the bar or in the alleys to either side. Lenny is definitely inside."

"Right then," Percy said. "Shall we go inside and see how this thing plays?"

Bud and Delilah nodded in unison, and Percy returned the gesture. He grabbed the handle and swung open the door. The three of them slowly eased their way inside the dimly lit bar.

Inside the bar, everything was quiet. Lenny was sitting at the bar, drinking what appeared to be a whiskey on the rocks. Beau looked up from the newspaper he was reading, and his face went pale. "Hey, guys. Listen. Lenny came in a few minutes ago and said he was meeting you to apologize for the tussle you had the other night. I hope that's okay. We aren't gonna have a repeat performance, are we?"

Bud shook his head, his eyes never leaving Lenny for a second. "It's all good, Beau. Nobody's gonna start swinging, right, Horowitz?"

Lenny looked up from his drink and nodded. "He's right, Beau. We're good here."

"Is there anybody else in the bar?" Delilah asked hopefully.

"Nope," Beau replied. "Just you four."

"Hey, Beau, could you do me a huge favor and give us some privacy? I'd owe you big time. Go turn over the door
sign to closed and take a smoke break so we can talk, okay?"

Beau nodded, looking at the group nervously. He hesitated for a moment, but then did as Bud asked. Turning the sign, he slipped into the back, and the group waited until they heard the metal bar of the side door click, then the door open and shut again. Once they were certain Beau was outside, Bud was the first to speak.

"So, Mr. Horowitz, we're here. If you want our help, I suggest you start talking."

"Before I tell you what I know, I want you to promise that you'll help me get out of here and as far away from that psychopath as possible."

"That will depend on your level of cooperation, Lenny."

"Trust me, Bud, you'll have my full cooperation. Now, come and have a drink with me, and I'll tell you everything."

"Sorry, boss, but I've recently been given a violent shove back onto the wagon, but I'll come and sit with you just the same."

Bud took a step towards the bar, and Percy put out his arm to his charge's chest, halting him. He looked at Bud with a grim look and slowly shook his head. When Bud saw the look in the angel's eyes, he understood without a single word being passed between them. Something was off about the situation.

"Oh, come on, Percy," Horowitz cooed. "That's no way to treat an old friend, is it?"

"You're no friend of ours anymore," Percy snapped. "I could smell your foul odor the minute we walked into the bar. I was merely waiting to see if Bud would notice it, too. I guess I have my answer. I'm going to give you one chance to tell us where Novikoff is, Mammon, and we'll gladly send you to rejoin your master."

"Mammon?" Bud asked, taken aback by the name. You mean like Mammon from the bible? The demon of greed?" "The same," Percy answered.

"Horowitz was easy to possess. He didn't even really put up a fight. He had so much wanting in his being to have everything that it almost gave me a hard-on when I took over his meat suit. He's long dead, of course, but hey, shit happens." The body that had once belonged to Lenny Horowitz rose from its stool. "Now, obviously, this is gonna end badly for you three, so let's get on with it, shall we?" Mammon made Lenny's face grin in an unnaturally wide curve that was sickening for Bud to behold. "Which one of you wants to die first?" The voice was no longer Lenny's. It was deep and distorted, guttural and animalistic. Bud was shaken and had to step back. Percy and Delilah stepped in front of him.

From over their shoulders, Bud watched in disbelief as the shell of skin, muscle, sinew, and blood was burned away in a flash of white-hot flames. The smell was atrocious, and Bud gagged slightly as it entered his nostrils. He covered his nose with the sleeve of the jacket he was wearing, but it didn't help. Once Mammon had released his true form, Bud could have sworn that the demon grew to twice Lenny's height. It was enormous and heavily muscled. Its skin was a deep red, like coagulated blood, and it had a tuft of jet-black fur running from the nape of its neck to the tip of its stubby tail. A gaping mouth of yellowed, jagged teeth dripped with thick ropes of saliva, and two onyx-colored horns jutted out about six inches from the top of its head.

It was the most frightening and grotesque sight that Bud had ever witnessed in his entire life.

Upon revealing himself, Mammon looked to the front door of the bar. There was an audible clicking sound both behind Bud and from the kitchen area. "Can't have you leaving before we're done, can we?"

Bud somehow knew the doors had just been magically locked and that there was no way out now. He instinctively grabbed his sidearm and pointed it at the monstrous figure.

"Now what do you think you're going to do with that, other than piss me off?" Mammon said in a venomous tone. "You insignificant little slug. Novikoff was right to send me to end you. You three aren't even worth his time."

"So he's not here," Percy said. "Where is he, beast?"

"Oh, make no mistake," Mammon replied. "He's watching from afar. This massacre will be too good not to witness."

"If you're done flapping your cock holster, shithead, can we get on with the part where we kick your ass all the way back to hell?" Delilah quipped.

"As you wish, traitorous whore," Mammon spat.

Bud watched in awe as Delilah and Percy dropped their visages once again, revealing the awesome beings hidden underneath. Percy's alabaster wings spread wide and then tucked back against his body. His eyes shone more brightly than the first time Bud had seen them, and his torso rippled with great cords of thick muscle. Delilah let out a terrifying howl as she once again transformed into the beautiful, but deadly, succubus that Bud remembered. However, this time, the aura she put forth was one of pure rage and hatred. The short, black claws protruding from her fingertips lengthened until they were several inches long, and fangs protracted from seemingly out of nowhere in her mouth. They reminded Bud of those he had seen in so many vampire movies.

Immediately after the spectacle, Mammon put on one of

his own. Bud watched in horror as the demon cut his own wrists with a long, black nail of his own, causing a heavy stream of purplish-colored blood to flow freely. He then flung the blood in all directions, on the floor and over the tables and chairs. Seconds later, thick gray shadows began to materialize all around the monster. The figures loosely resembled the Grim Reaper, faceless beneath hooded cloaks, and moaning as if carrying the weight of all the ages on their incorporeal shoulders. Mammon raised his arms towards the three, and the shadows began to advance. Bud steadied himself, Delilah and Percy visibly tensed, and the fight commenced.

The shadows were the first to act. They advanced on the group, gliding across the floor until they popped up right in front of them. Two of them attacked Delilah, materializing what looked like daggers made of shadow out of thin air. They each took a swipe at her, but she was too quick for them and dodged out of the way. The daggers narrowly missed her, and she took such a quick step back that Bud hadn't even realized her back was now directly in front of him. "Cover your ears!" she yelled back to Bud. He did so, and she took in a deep breath. On the exhale, she let out such a booming, blood-curdling shriek that Bud thought she might bring the ceiling of the bar down on top of them. The shadows were blown back from the sheer force of it and had to regroup. As Bud watched them struggle, he took a couple of shots at the shadow creatures with his pistol, but it was no use. The bullets went straight through them with only a whisp of black mist floating away from their forms.

Bud turned his head just in time to see Percy backed into one of the near corners with three shadows advancing on him. He had a slight smirk on his face as they approached, waiting until they were almost on top of him to act. They drew their daggers and raised them, poised to strike, but Percy beat them to the attack. He began to hover about six inches above the ground, wings spread wide. His eyes, mouth, and nostrils filled with a brilliant yellowish light, and he sent the beam that emerged blasting directly into his opponents. The three assailants let out what would most likely equate to a shriek of pain and then disintegrated into nothingness. He wheeled on the other two that had attacked Delilah, his eyes bright with rage. However, before he could make a move on them, Delilah executed a perfect front flip, landing a few feet away from them, and blew a purplish flame of what Bud thought looked like dragon's fire into the creatures, and they met the same fate as their comrades.

Mammon stood in wait, watching his minions fall without so much as a hint of concern for their losses. He looked around him, watching more of the shadow creatures come up from the spots where he had flung his blood. He smiled his sickening smile as even more of the creatures came up to challenge the three allies. This time, there were at least a dozen. Percy shot Delilah a look of concern; she shot back a crazed smile, and they went into the fray once more.

Percy folded his wings in front of himself slightly, bringing the tips to his hands, and in one fluid motion, he plucked two feathers from his wingtips that instantly formed into ivory-handled daggers. Delilah materialized a black leather whip that had to be at least ten feet in length, and swirled it about her head. When she brought it down, it rang out through the room with a loud crack that shook Bud to his core. They both danced in amongst the shadows, weaving back and forth in almost perfect unison, cutting down foes as they went.

Bud surveyed the room and noticed that none of the shadow creatures were targeting him. Neither was Mammon. His attention was solely on Bud's two new friends. Bud saw the opening he thought he needed. He raised his pistol, unloading several rounds in the direction of Mammon. Two of the rounds missed as Mammon shifted just as Bud fired. The other two rounds didn't. One bullet smacked into the demon's left shoulder, and the other grazed him in the ribs. Mammon let out a howl of pain and anger, whipping his head around to peer at Bud. He growled a sadistic growl and said, "You insignificant little sack of shit! How dare you attack me?"

Before any of them could react, Mammon lept across three of the bar tables, landed directly in front of Bud, and grabbed him by the throat. Lifting him into the air with one hand, he used the other to rip open Bud's shirt, exposing his torso. "You think you know pain? You think you know loss? You think you know suffering? You know nothing! I will teach you before this is over," Mammon cooed. He then ran a razor-sharp claw down Bud's chest from his clavicles to his navel, leaving a deep gash that trickled crimson liquid as Bud howled in agony from the wound.

Percy looked back in time to see the exchange. "No!" he cried out in fury. "Bud! No!" But there was nothing he could do. If he went to Bud now, the shadow creatures would follow, making Bud's current predicament even worse. He and Delilah had to hold them off for him. "Bud!" Percy cried out again while dodging a blow from a shadow dagger. "Bud, draw on your strength! Do it now before it's too late! You have to feel it! Make it come to you!"

"He'd better do something fast, Percy. More of those things are pouring out of the floor!" Delilah added. "Anytime now, sweetheart!" she yelled to Bud—more and more of the shadow creatures manifested from the dark. Soon, Percy and Delilah would be overwhelmed, and it would all be over.

Mammon tightened his grip on Bud's throat, making it nearly impossible for the man to breathe.

"Strength? What strength does an ant have under the hoof of the bull? What strength do you have, Mr. Barrett?" Mammon asked mockingly. "Would it be the same strength that allowed Novikoff to torture and mutilate your cunt wife? The strength that allowed him to use your little bitch daughter for a pin cushion and a play toy before putting an end to her miserable little life? You have no strength, mortal, and very soon, the light will leave you, just as your supposed strength did the day you let your family die."

Bud felt a sudden burning from deep within his chest and stomach. A white-hot rage that began to boil up from deep inside. He suddenly grabbed onto the wrist that Mammon was holding him with, and the demon looked down with surprise to see his skin starting to smoke. A twinge of fear began to fester behind the demon's eyes, as Bud's began to glow with a fiery white light, much the same as Percy's. The fear settled in further for the beast as Bud squeezed down harder on the hand, wrenched himself free, and with one swift motion, snapped it like a twig. The demon of greed screamed in agony over his destroyed wrist as Bud placed both hands into his chest and pushed. The monster flew backwards with such force that he went through the wall behind the bar, taking broken bottles of liquor with him.

It was Bud's turn to advance now. Months of frustration flowed through his mind, along with images of Susan and Lilly. His hands began to glow with the same white light filling his eyes. Percy and Delilah watched in amazement as he bounded into the air, landing on the demon's chest, pinning down its arms with his knees. That's when they saw it. Bud raised his arms over his head, and an alabaster sword of pure light began to fill them. It was the sword of Michael. Bud looked down at Mammon's unbelieving face, taking in the look of fear he was sure the demon had never experienced before. In an almost disembodied voice, Bud said to the creature, "Tell your master, after I send you to him, that I am coming for his essence, that I will find it, and I will take it. Tell him that there's not a damn thing he can do about it. Novikoff will follow you shortly, filth." Before Mammon could react, Bud swung the blade down in a huge, sweeping arc and released Mammon's head from his body.

As if sensing their leader's impending defeat even before Bud's stroke fell, the remaining shadow creatures quickly fled back into the shadows from whence they had first appeared. Bud's eyes were still glowing as he stood up and looked back at Percy and Delilah. They were both covered in sweat, cuts, and scrapes, but were mostly intact. They smiled at him, bowing their heads to him slightly in recognition. Not a word was spoken between them. Bud looked back down to the spot where Mammon had been slain. The creature's body began to smoke, spark, and then burst into flame. A few moments later, only ashes remained. Bud stepped back and looked around him, his eyes finally returning to normal, and the sword of Michael disappearing back into the ether. He walked over and rejoined his friends.

"Well, that didn't go exactly as planned," Percy said sarcastically. "That being said, it looks like you found your strength and faith again, Bud."

"Fuck that!" Delilah squealed. "You kicked his fucking ass!" She began to bounce slightly and clap her hands in approval.

"Delilah," Percy said.

"Oh, lighten up, tight ass," Delilah shot back at the angel.
She looked sidelong at Bud and gave a coy wink and a grin.

"What's next?" Bud asked Percy. "Do we go after Novikoff?"

"Yes, Mr. Barrett, we do. But not just yet. This is going to be tougher than we imagined. We're gonna need some help, and Jehovah spoke to me just as the fight ended. He has held council with the other

two gods. Bud, two more people have been called to
your aid. We have a trip to take."

Chapter 18

The three of them sat at the bar with the thousand-yard stares of a group of Vietnam-era war veterans, none of them uttering a single word. Each was nursing a drink, their eyes fixed downward. In kind, Beau himself was staring wordlessly, but not into nothingness. He was too busy looking at what was left of the inside of his bar. Chairs and tables had been splintered, glasses and bottles had been shattered, and somehow, there were burn marks everywhere without even the slightest hint that a fire had broken out. He had heard the commotion from outside, of course, but when he tried to get back into his bar, the door to the employee entrance was inexplicably stuck closed, and no matter how hard he tried to force his way in, it wouldn't budge.

After a few minutes that felt like an eternity, the door just as inexplicably swung open without a single hint that it had ever been stuck in the first place. Now here he stood behind the bar, pouring drinks for the four of them, wondering what the fuck had happened to his life's dream. Almost as if he had heard his thoughts, Bud spoke up and said flatly to his long-time friend, "Beau, old buddy, there are some things that should be left unexplained."

Beau just stared through him, still gazing at the mess, and feeling that these would be the last three patrons of his establishment for a very long time. "Really?" he asked, unsure of how else to respond. "Really, Bud? You don't think that my knowing how my bar got utterly destroyed in the span of a few minutes is important?"

"At current, no," Bud said flatly. "Maybe one day, but not today."

"I assume you are worried about the repairs and bills that will go along with them?" Percy interjected.

"That's an understatement," Delilah added, a hint of a smile playing at her lips.

"Delilah," Percy interrupted. "Not the time." He looked at her in a way that was both kind and with a hint of how a parent might look at a child who is about to say something that needs not to be said. "Mr. McCormick, I assure you that I have connections that will render this a non-issue very shortly and that you will absolutely incur no cost. It will be completely covered. I have already contacted them, and they'll arrive the day after tomorrow. You will also be compensated for your lack of business for those two days."

Now it was Bud's turn to look flabbergasted. "Now you wanna tell me just how the hell you plan on pulling that off, Percy?"

"Not to worry, Bud. As the old expression goes, it's not what you know, it's who you know."

Delilah snorted out a short laugh and then added, "You can say that again, P."

Bud eyed the pair for a moment suspiciously and then turned his attention back to his old friend. "Beau, you and I go back for years, so I don't want to keep you in the dark about what happened here tonight, but I'm not sure you could handle the truth." Still looking at his long-time friend, Bud said to the open air, "What do you think, Percy?"

"Well, as I stated earlier, we do need as many allies as we can get right now, so it may not be a bad idea to fill him in if you think he can withstand the initial shock."

"Initial shock of what?" Beau asked in a confused tone. "What the hell is this Brit talking about, Bud?

"Do you trust me, Beau?" Bud asked solemnly.

"You know I do, Bud."

"Show him, Percy."

"Ah shit! Here we go!" Delilah added playfully.

Percy approached Beau, and before he could protest or ask any other questions, Percy touched two fingers to Beau's forehead and then caught him as he collapsed. When he regained consciousness, the three of them explained the current state of affairs. Beau sat listening, transfixed to their every word. When they were finished, they swore him to secrecy. They also asked him to be their eyes and ears in the area for any suspicious activity that even slightly twinged the hairs on the back of his neck. "You know I will, Bud," Beau had responded. "You're my friend, Bud, and since these other two are with you now, they are my friends as well."

"So there it is, Beau," Bud said plainly. Percy will have his guys come and fix up your place, and you'll keep your ear to the ground for us."

"Sure thing, Bud," Beau said warmly. "Sounds like these bastards deserve what's coming to them. I hope you fry the son of a bitch."

"Now that's my kind of thinking," Delilah said to Beau with a wink. Percy just glared at her for a moment and then rolled his eyes with a slight grin and a shake of his head.

Bud spoke up again. "Hey, Beau, I was wondering about something."

"What's that?" Beau responded.

"Do you remember me coming in here the weekend when Mya and Charlie were..." He paused for a long moment. Beau stood uncomfortably behind the bar, pouring his friend another drink, and Percy and Delilah both looked away. "The night of the massacre," Bud finally stated.

"Sure, Bud, I remember," Beau replied evenly. "You looked pretty rough, like you hadn't slept in a month."

"Beau, something's been bothering me about that weekend, and I need to know. How much did I have to drink that night?

Beau looked at Bud, a little confused. "I don't understand," he said after a moment of thought. "Bud, you weren't drinking that night, well, at least not alcohol. You initially came in, ordered a shot, stared at it for a few minutes, and then asked me to take it for you because you had changed your mind. You talked about being stressed, but then said Susan and Lily would be ashamed, so you asked for a diet soda instead. I poured it, and then you got up to go to the bath..." His words hitched in his throat. He then got a disturbed look on his face like he was remembering something unpleasant and said, "Oh shit! How the fuck could I have forgotten that?!"

"Forgotten what?" Bud said, his voice becoming both shaky and heated.

Beau continued, "A man was sitting beside you when you got up to go to the head that night. I thought he looked a little suspicious because he stared at you all the way to the bathroom hallway until you were out of sight. I thought about mentioning it to you as soon as you got back, but I must have spaced out for a second because when I snapped out of it, the man was gone. I must have gotten busy after you came out, because I forgot to tell you. Jesus, Bud, I'm sorry."

"Fuck!" Bud barked. I fucking knew it! Someone must have fucking drugged me that night. That's why I was out so long, not because I went on a fucking bender!"

"But you looked fine when you left," Beau argued.

"Not all knock-out drugs take effect immediately," Bud retorted.

Beau looked absolutely sick with himself and turned pale. He dropped his head, and Bud noticed. "Hey, Beau, it's not your fault, man. Don't worry about it. It's in the past. You couldn't have known. The bastard must have been working with Novikoff." He shakily stood up and put his hand on Beau's shoulder to comfort him.

Beau said, "Fuck, Bud, I'm still so sorry. What can I do?"

"Do you remember what the man looked like, Beau?" Percy chimed in.

"I do now, Percy," Beau replied. "When I was stuck outside during the scrum you guys were having in here, it's like a haze was lifted and I could think more clearly. That's how I remembered the guy just now. It came back to me almost right away."

"Must have happened when Bud ass-fucked Old Red Sack," Delilah quipped with a giggle. "The power shift lifted whatever veil was over the bar."

"Indeed," Percy added. "But please, Delilah, your language, dear." Delilah stuck out her tongue at him, mocking the words, "your language, dear," back at him. Percy shook his head and continued. "So, Beau, the description, if you please."

Beau grinned at Delilah for a moment, who made a kissy face back at him. "The man was tall, slender, and had a rat-like face. Looked like a weasel, to be honest. He had slicked back black hair, Van Dyke beard, and..." He paused to think. "Yeah! That's right! I remember he smiled at me once, and I thought it was funny that his upper front two teeth were gold."

"Klein!" Percy said, his voice slightly growling. Bud jerked his head to look at the angel because he had never seen him this annoyed. Percy continued, "That rat bastard! He definitely drugged you, Bud!"

"How do you know?" Bud asked, a little confused.

Delilah spoke up because Percy was too busy fuming to speak. "Percy and this Klein fella have history. He was a Nazi back during the war, and back in the day, he had a particular hard-on for killing Jews—his favorite M.O. was poisoning them by slipping them a Mickey. Percy had several run-ins with him because not only did P. catch him in the act one time and Klein got away, but he was also helping the away team search for the lost essences. He actually succeeded in helping them find one after he tortured a young Jewish boy in Brooklyn for the intel. Also, calling him a rat bastard is more accurate than you know. The walking shit-stain is a Wererat-a shifter."

Beau looked stunned at this new information while Bud shook his head and muttered, "For fuck sake! Could my life possibly get any fucking weirder?"

"Careful what you wish for, handsome," Delilah cooed to Bud.

Percy finally gathered himself and said through gritted teeth, "Friends, I believe we should find out where Mr. Klein is and pay him a visit."

"Agreed," Bud replied, giving Percy a light wrap on his upper arm. "Where do we start?"

Chapter 19

His day's task complete, Marcus Klein crept nearer to the abandoned shack, formerly a strip club, on Heyman Street, casting glances back over his shoulders the entire way. He knew full well that just because you couldn't see anyone, it didn't mean that you weren't being followed. Years of an opportunistic lifestyle, paired with his shifter abilities as a Wererat, had afforded him the luxury to pretty much pass unseen if he chose. Over time, he had perfected it to the point of making it more of an art form than a skill. It had gotten him out of many scrapes in the past and had also allowed him to cause many. Most people didn't understand the satisfaction of sneaking up on some poor, unsuspecting jerk that had it coming, and then sliding a freshly sharpened blade between his ribs.

Yes, the shadows were his friend and confidant. The one loyal thing he had in his life. So he was completely surprised when he heard a voice emerge from the same darkness that usually protected him so well. It was a *woman's* voice. He thought, "Wait a minute. Maybe this won't be such a bad encounter after all." His enthusiasm was short-lived.

"Turn around slowly, dick breath," he heard the woman say with obvious contempt in her tone.

He tried to think on his feet. How had she gotten the drop on him? He was scrambling to think of something clever to say to smooth over the situation as he turned, but much to his chagrin, the situation escalated before he could get out a single word. There, standing with the woman, were one man who looked vaguely familiar to him and another he was sure he knew. It was Percy, that goodie-two-shoes prick angel, who had spoiled his fun on more than one occasion, and none of the three looked happy at all.

Klein gave his widest smile. "Percy, old boy, how have you been?" he asked in a sickeningly sweet tone. He had his arms raised in a mock-surrender position.

In a move so uncharacteristic of Percy that both Delilah and Bud looked on with shocked disbelief, Percy walked up to the man and socked him hard in the gut without saying a word. Klein dropped to the gravel. Percy picked the man up from the ground and punched him in the gut again, causing Klein to topple again. The angel picked him up for a third time, preparing to hit Klein yet again, when Bud intervened.

"That's enough, Percy," Bud commanded. Percy drew back to swing. "That's enough, Percy! Damn it!" The angel feigned another strike, making Klein flinch, but halted his movement and sat Klein down hard on his feet. Percy spat at the Wererat's shoes. The sneer Percy had on his face told Marcus all he needed to know. Percy would have probably beaten him to death if the stranger hadn't stopped him. Again, his thankfulness was brief. He sucked in a few short, ragged breaths and said, "What the fuck was that for?" like he didn't already know.

"Your very existence, you piece of trash," Percy snarled, burning a hole through Klein with his gaze.

"I should fucking obliterate you where you stand after what you did to me," Bud said through gritted teeth. "And I will, just as soon as you tell me where Novikoff is."

"That's not very good motivation to snitch, now is it?" Klein said flatly, yet with a slight tremor in his tone.

Percy started to step toward Klein again, but Delilah put her arm on Percy's chest and stopped him. "Easy, Tiger," she quipped. "Let our baby bird try to fly."

"I'm only gonna ask you one more time, you filthy waste of space, and then I'm gonna..." Klein cut off Bud's threat.

"Let me stop you right there, Cowboy," Klein hissed suddenly. He was unbelievably smiling for some reason Bud couldn't figure out. "Novikoff knows you survived, and he's not in the least bit happy about it, but don't you worry. He's gonna fix that up quick, fast, and in a hurry. Currently, he has bigger fish to fry, though. Once he's done with his business in California, you, the tight ass, and the slut are done. That is, if my boys and I don't do the job for him." He grinned widely.

"What the fuck are you talking about, you walking cleanup rag?" Delilah asked, her patience wearing thin.

"You didn't think I was at this joint all by my lonesome, now did ya?" Klein chirped. He whistled loudly.

From inside the bar, animalistic growls and grunts could be heard. Bud's eyes widened as the back door to the building was busted out with such force that it reminded him of a grenade going off.

Three huge silhouettes could be seen filling the open jam. Simultaneously, audible cracks and pops began coming from Klein's slender frame. He groaned slightly as his face began to twist and contort, and his nose elongated into a hairy snout. His back became slightly more hunched and thicker, coarse white hair patched his arms and legs, which had unceremoniously ripped open his suit. His fingernails became razor-sharp, and a worm-like pink tail burst forth from the seat of his pants. Klein had shifted. His ruby eyes now glowed with a burning hatred for the three companions. He looked back at the doorway and smiled. The shadows emerged from the doorway that now seemed more like a portal to hell. The first to present was a large humanoid figure, the visage of a gigantic, mutated wolf with a jet-black coat of fur. Next, a slightly shorter but even more heavily muscled figure emerged with the head of a strange-looking boar. To round out the misfit three musketeers, as Bud's mind imagined them to be, was a man with the features of a huge grey cat.

"Holy fuck!" Delilah began, feigning fear. "Percy, I'm scared...of how ridiculously ugly these motherfuckers are! With mugs like that, I bet you never get any pussy, am I right?" she teased through a laugh.

"Eat it, cunt!" The werewolf huffed.

"Sorry, Fido, I don't care for cocktail weiners!" she yelled back. Then, pointing at Bud's crotch, she added, "I prefer footlongs!"

The four musclebound horrors growled and charged. Percy and Delilah dropped their glamours and returned the advance. Bud took a deep breath, focused, let out a primal scream of anger, and...nothing happened. Not a single thing. He stood there, shocked, not knowing why he wasn't able to draw out the light inside of him as he had done against the demon, Mammon, inside Beau's Place. He frantically tried again and again to summon the feeling of absolute power, but still, it would spring up to meet him. Then he remembered his sidearm. Before they had left to find Klein, Percy had taken him to the alley hangout of an old peddler, whom he had known for several years, who just so happened to deal in small-time supernatural weapons. Percy had acquired two magazines of silver-tipped bullets for Bud's particular caliber. He drew the black matte handgun into its natural firing position and began advancing with his friends.

Delilah was the first to meet combat. Her huge onyx wings flapped a couple of times, and she glided effortlessly over to cut off the wolf. From her back, she drew two purplish-tinted stilettos with silver-edged blades; another of Percy's purchases from his merchant friend. The wolf raised his arms, thick with bulky muscles, and swiped at Delliah with his razor-sharp black claws. Delilah spun out of the way with the grace of a ballet dancer, and as she came around, she sank one of the blades into the back of her opponent. The werewolf yelped with pain and then turned to Delilah. She had already turned back to face him, a sly grin on her face. "What's wrong, Lassie? Did Timmy fall down the well?" The wolf let out a deafening howl and leaped at the succubus suddenly. Again, Delilah was ready. While the canine horror was still mid-jump, Delilah also bounded up to meet him.

However, she purposely took a lower angle and came up underneath him. She savagely thrust upward, jamming her blade directly into the creature's abdomen, before landing behind him effortlessly on her feet. The wolf went limp in the air and thudded heavily to the ground, skidding several feet and coming to a stop, and lay motionless from the wound that was inflicted.

Percy, not to be outdone by his cohort, was in the midst of a spectacular dustup with the boar. The beast had even momentarily managed to get the upper hand on the guardian angel until Percy had jumped back, and with a huge flap of his alabaster wings, had thrown thick clouds of dust and dirt into the monster's eyes. The porcine terror squealed and grunted with rage at this offense and blindly charged the angel, intent on goring him. Percy sidestepped the advance, and the boar blew right past him. However, the angel's shift had cost him in the end because the werecat had shifted into its own position, grabbing Percy in a bear hug. It growled loudly and plunged its fangs into Percy's shoulder.

Percy grimaced and let out a sharp bellow of pain. Just as the werecat opened its mouth for a second bite, a silver bullet blew blood, grey matter, and bone through the back of its head. The creature slumped to the ground, and as the wereboar advanced on Percy again, the usually reserved Brit pulled a silver scimitar from a sheath on his hip and decapitated his foe.

All three of the companions turned their attention back to Klein, who was still standing in the same spot as when the fight had commenced. He instantly shifted back to his more human form and put up his hands in surrender. Unphased and unchanged, the three of them came up to the Wererat and stared a hole through him. As he attempted to speak, the only words he got out were, "Come on, guys, we can talk about t..." As he said it, Bud thrust the muzzle of his pistol into Klein's mouth.

"You are part of the reason my partner and boss are dead, and that I wasn't there to help them when they needed me." Bud pulled the trigger, and Klein's body slumped to the ground. Bud turned away, a cold and distant look filling his eyes.

"Thank you for the assist, Bud," Percy said in his usual matter-of-fact way. However, even as he said it, he was wincing from Delilah applying a clean handkerchief to his bite wound.

"What do we do now?" Bud asked. "And why the fuck couldn't I summon my superpowers as I did back at Beau's?"

Percy replied, "That I don't know, but what I do know is that Klein must have somehow learned about the girl. He mentioned California. That's where one of the two people Jehovah revealed to me lives. We cannot allow this girl to come to harm before she's ready to assist in your cause, Bud. Just like you, she clearly isn't ready for what's coming. We have to get to her before the Russian."

"Fine," Bud said flatly. "Let's move."

"Not so fast, Cowboy," Delilah interrupted. "I saw you back there just now. You couldn't get it up. You wanna end up like Old McDonald's farm friends here?" She gestured to Klein.

"Well, we sure as shit can't let Novikoff get to her while I'm figuring out what the fuck," Bud shot back, a little more sharply than intended.

"No, we can't," Percy said. "Delilah, I want you to get out to California and get to this girl. Convince her to leave with you before Novikoff tracks her down."

"What?!" Bud spat out at Percy. "Are you insane? We can't let Delilah go out there by herself. What if she runs into that prick? She can't take him alone!"

"Aww, shucks," Delilah teased. "It's almost like you care about me or somethin, Buddy boy."

"We're wasting time," Percy said mildly. "Get moving, dear."

"What about Bud's issue?" Delilah asked. This time, there was no sarcasm or playfulness in her tone.

"You let me worry about that," Percy answered. "I have a friend in New Orleans who might be able to help us figure that out. Go collect the girl and meet us there on Bourbon Street. You know how to reach me once you've arrived."

"Wait," Delilah interjected. "You're not talking about Remy, are you?! Is he the third?"

Percy looked at her blankly and nodded. "He is."

"Holy fuck! This is about to get really interesting. That Cajun bastard is as crazy as a rat in a tin shithouse. Okay. I'm out of here!" With that, Delilah unfurled her wings and, with a mighty flap, soared high into the sky.

The last thing she heard before ascending out of hearing range was Bud's voice yelling to Percy, "Wait! Who the fuck is Remy?"

Epilogue

Los Angeles, California

Amy stood lazily behind the counter of Spooks and Spells Apothecary and Wicca Supply Shop. No one had been in for almost three hours, and the teenage girl was getting restless. She reached into her charge case and pulled out the little black earbuds. Placing them in her ears and grabbing her phone, she turned on Bluetooth and paired her device. She scrolled through her music until she found a song to match her mood. "This one," she thought, and pressed play. Mudvayne's "Dig" slammed into the small bones of her inner ears. "Much better," she mumbled. She grabbed up her copy of Buckland's Complete Book of Witchcraft and began to flip mindlessly through the pages.

She had a lot on her mind for someone who was barely eighteen. She had lost her parents in a tragic car accident two years ago and was still haunted by the loss. While she had seemingly dealt with their deaths as well as any sixteen-year-old child could in her predicament, being an orphan sucked, she surmised. Not having parents to tell her goodnight, take her for random ice cream trips, or walk her down the aisle one day, sucked even harder. The only comfort she had was found in her older sister, Jane. Jane was nineteen at the time of the accident, three years older than Amy, and since the pair didn't have any close living relatives to care for them, the state had awarded custody of Amy to her big sister.

This was fine with Amy, as she had always looked up to Jane, anyway. Jane was the one who got her into practicing Wicca, telling her that she needed a positive outlet for her grief. Amy ran with the idea. She had thrown herself passionately into the arts of light and white magic, working on small rituals and spells to help bless her big sister and her friends with good fortune and good health. It was her way of trying to protect others against the pain and tragedy she had experienced at such a young age. She enjoyed Wicca so much that, recently, she had even tried to cast a few more powerful protection and healing spells, but didn't have much luck. She had set her mind to keep trying, because if there was one thing she was, it was persistent.

At the current moment, however, none of that mattered. It was just a week ago that Jane came to her and gave her news she hadn't been ready to hear. Jane sat her down and had a long discussion about both of their futures. Amy sat on the edge of her bed, silent, as Jane told her that since she was of age now, she would be leaving Amy for the fall and winter to start college in San Francisco. When Amy asked why she had to go, Jane explained that it wasn't because she didn't want to be with her, but because, when their parents died, she had put her plans on hold to care for her little sister. Amy had gotten angry at first, yelling at Jane that she didn't care about her, and her leaving proved that. After she had a chance to calm down, however, Amy apologized to Jane and said she understood. She expressed in great detail how much she hated it, but said that she understood.

Before Jane left, she took some of the life insurance money the sisters had gotten from their parents' accident and set Amy up with a small efficiency apartment in a decent neighborhood. She also got set up with a job working for one of Jane's friends, who owned a small Wicca supply shop within walking distance of her apartment. So while she begrudged her sister for leaving, she was happy for the modicum of independence that living alone brought to her. She was making her own money, paying her own bills, and living a fairly normal life. She was single, but that might change soon: her boss had a younger sister Amy's age, and she had promised to introduce them.

Amy came out of her trance just as Mudvayne's song "Happy?" came to an end, and the little rusty bell above the shop's front door jingled pitifully. A clearly female form walked into view around one of the shelves of potion ingredients and up to the front counter. She was wearing a navy-blue hoodie pulled in close around her face, and when she threw it back, Amy's first thought was, "Damn, this chick is hot." She kept that thought to herself, though. She had long, toned legs that practically reached up to her neck, which were covered with black fishnet stockings. She had a larger-than-normal bust for someone of her petite build, covered with a skin-tight baby tee. Her milky skin stood in stark contrast to Amy's mocha-colored skin, and her long, jet-black hair was naturally wavy and beautiful. Amy shook the cobwebs loose and spoke.

"Can I help you, miss?" she asked in her best customer service voice.

"Maybe. Maybe not. Are you Amy Jackson?" the lady asked in response with a thick accent Amy swore she had heard on a rerun of the reality show Jersey Shore.

"Depends on who's asking," Amy snapped back, a little shorter than she meant to.

"My kind of girl," the lady chuckled. "Good for you, doll," she added with a sly grin.

"Name's Delilah, love, and boy do I have a fucking story for you."